MW01136683

crown

crown

A Novel

evanthia bromiley

Grove Press
New York

FIRST EDITION

Published simultaneously in Canada
Printed in the United States of America

This book was set in 11-pt. Berling
by Alpha Design & Composition of Pittsfield, NH.

First Grove Atlantic hardcover edition: June 2025

Library of Congress Cataloging-in-Publication data is available for this title.

ISBN 978-0-8021-6462-9
eISBN 978-0-8021-6463-6

Grove Press
an imprint of Grove Atlantic
154 West 14th Street
New York, NY 10011

Distributed by Publishers Group West

groveatlantic.com

25 26 27 28   10 9 8 7 6 5 4 3 2 1

For Sean and Althea

dramatis personae

VIRGINIA WOODS—energy, movement

EVAN WOODS—architect of daydreams, cloud-watcher

JUDE WOODS—poet and pregnant packer of boxes, mother of Evan and Virginia

YOU—float-flying on the other side of skin, blood, water—

MEN (Various)—extracurricular, sex

THE SLEEPLESS MAN—watcher-over of small growing things

eviction

virginia woods

The sun sinks low as I follow my brother up the deer path from the river. We slash through reed and cattail taller than our heads and climb. Sagebrush explodes with little brown birds at the top and we don't stop, we don't say anything when we see the sheriff's car crawling slow on the dirt road below. In the dusk atop the ridge my brother is now a sliver, watching the car, then I break trail and we barrel down, kicking up chert and stone. At the base of the ridge, land flattens and greens. There is tall grass ahead, clean and fresh and loaded with seedheads, and in the center of the field are the trailers.

Thirty-five white rectangles, each with its own stoop and naked window. Built on fixed steel chassis, they sag in white vinyl with metal roofs. As we pass into the park the neighbors seem not to see us—the old woman who grows roses and talks too much, the army vet who did five tours in Iraq and doesn't talk at all, and the old man in guayabera and hat of battered straw. It is only the Sleepless Man who watches us, smoking and wide-awake, his twelve-gauge shotgun leaning beside him on the stoop and his eyes glittering like bottle glass.

By the time the cruiser parks in front of 565 we've reached the deep shade of the cottonwood tree, and Evan strips off his shirt and sneakers and begins to climb, even as the sheriff steps out of the car and our mama stands on the stoop to meet him.

I say a warning:

Evan.

The wind lifts, and leaves go musical above.

Evan.

He climbs. Straight up the tree. Leaf-shadow strikes my twin's bare chest and back and legs. Evan is a good climber. Above, the branches hold armfuls of sky and the blades of my brother's shoulders shine like maybe they are wings. I stay where I am, listening to the

tick   tick   tick

of the sheriff's engine.

jude woods

M iss Jude Woods?
       Yes.

This your residence, 565 Hermosa Meadows?

Yes.

Not far from the river out here, are you? Trees that big.

No. Not far.

The sheriff moves one foot neatly alongside the other. Red dirt scuffed on the toes. He says:

I would imagine you got the notice in the mail.

How long? I ask.

Three days.

All right then.

I do apologize, Miss Woods, but I'm going to need to adhere this eviction notice to the door.

We trade places. I take my big belly down into the red dirt. Behind him through the screen lies the chaos of my kitchen, where the twins have torn in and out all day. No. Not mine. Got to stop that, thinking of it as mine.

Ma'am?

Yes.

You got a baby on the way. And I know from the paperwork there's two others. Ten-year-old twins.

Nine.

Sorry?

They're nine.

You got a place to go? With the kids?

Yes. Of course.

Where's that, then?

I lift the mass of hair from my neck. There is a breeze; it is hard to feel but it is there.

You all got to go get some kind of roof over your heads. You need assistance, I can help find that. We might go back to the office. Fill out some paperwork.

I feel the watching eyes of the park. The sun is setting at such an angle as to turn every bit of glass, windows and windshields, molten. I like at night how the naked windows show each trailer's bright heart, lit up from the inside and how all the human ordinariness is exposed. I especially like it when those inside love, when they fight.

There's the shelter, says the sheriff.

I touch the old scar, the one from where they were birthed. I feel the hard ridge of it through thin cotton. Everything I love in this world has been cut from me and this place will be no different.

Y ou climb into June. Everything green and growing and splitting open. Even the air is green, a green wind moving the branches in slow creaks, flattening the grass below. There is green rushing in the deep of the river and bursting in the ditches, seeds. You are tucked tight inside Mama, like a seed.

Do you hear his voice? Telling us to go? Probably not. Baby ears all full of heartbeat and bloodrush. When you're grown a little, I will teach you how to climb. Climbing is easy: you notch fingers in grooves of bark and push off the ground, then leave it behind.

Up here leaves flip like the silver bellies of fish. Light bursts behind the leaves and the branches all crooked in the light. In the dark below, our sister is gold. V's hair is the glow of hay laid flat to dry and her eyes are the awake green of before it was cut.

All I see of Mama is the top of her head, the razor-straight part of her hair.

It's quiet up here.

But you have to be careful. Cottonwoods fall easy. Junk trees. Drop themselves into the ground to rot and feed everything else. Fallen, the dead trees are wider than I am tall. If you tightrope walk the trunks over still water you see peaks of red cliffs humped like sleeping animals below.

The notice on the door a white shout.

Uh-oh. Mama's turning now, her long haunch shifting, her black hair sliding over her shoulder like a muscle. She puts her body between the tree and him, us and him.

jude

Get out.

My words a lash. Now, I say, and the sheriff moves quick, stumbling a little on his own shined shoes. He's got to get by me to do what I'm asking and leave, but I track him. Get close. He makes it past without touching me, but just barely. Even once he's in the car, pressing a button, the slick glass rising, even once the car moves, I wide-step alongside the crackle of tires until the car reaches the cattleguard.

Virginia hurtles into me. Her lashes are white at their tips from sun. Colliding with Virginia is like trying to hold sunlight, caliche. Evan arrives more gently. Their architecture is the same but painted in a different palette.

Where will we go?

Evan's voice is cool and clipped: a snowflake settling on skin. He places the toe of one sneaker atop the other, and Virginia says,

You knew.

It'll be all right.

We don't have anywhere to go.

It'll be all right.

Virginia opens her mouth again and I put my finger over it.

To bed, I say and push them from me.

Dark is pooling now between the trailers and the field and purling in the river. The wish to lie in it. To let the darkness soak into me and also the quiet—but there are teeth in it too. There are the night things moving in the darkness and readying themselves in hunger and I am so tired. To bed, I say.

No.

Sixteen when I had them. The stucco of the clinic was bubblegum pink. The doctor holding one twin. The other clasped against my neck, small, breath-warm. A C-section, the doctor said. I was sixteen and there were two children on my chest. He said: Next time, when you go into labor—if there is a next time—get to the hospital right away. Do you understand?

I'm strong.

Not a matter of strength, he said.

There were two heartbeat babies on me. Explain again, I said—I remember looking into their wise and wrinkled faces—I'm listening. Talk of *rupture*, womb walls *weak*, tissue can *split* . . .

The three of us are simple. A girl opened with a knife. Twin one, raven-silent and dreaming. Twin two, shrieking, golden.

evan

You have a trick. You're visible from outside but invisible inside. Paddling around in there. I am a boy and V is a girl and right now, you are a fish slipping between us.

To bed, Mama says. But V is amped.

Cartwheeling and tossing one of those tiny rubber hands that you buy in a Grab Me machine at the door over and over. It's dirty. So the sticky hand won't stick. Holdstill, says Mama, trying to comb some tangle out of blonde, but V can't, so Mama gives up.

To bed.

I'm hot, V says.

Mama says, Arms up and peels the T-shirt from my sister. V parades across the room, flat-chested as me. She sports days-of-the-week panties: TUESDAY hanging out the top of her shorts. Friday, that's when the locksmith will change the locks. To bed, Mama says. We are sticky skin and sweat.

Lie with us.

It's so hot.

Lie with us, lie with us!

All right. For a minute. She lowers her body into the bed, careful because the baby. Virginia licks her shoulder. I say:

Play Find Her?

Ready or not! says V.

Ready or not, we each slap a hand (*careful, please*) where you are, where you might be—the magic is that you answer, not just one time but every time. You're on the other side of skin muscle water blood.

My sister presses her mouth against hard roundness and whispers:

We are here.

Twin eyes meet over Mama's enormousness. The pregnancy has grown her into something magic. A whale. A bear. A mountain.

We're here, I echo.

We hold our breath. Wait. Wait . . .

You rise.

All three of us feel the bulk of your moving, choosing. V squeals; Mama gasps. I smile. You fit your heel to my palm, half kick, half kiss. The baby chose you, Evan, Mama says, and kisses V. Then in the bed it is warm and good.

But V is asking an avalanche of questions: *Wherewillwe?*
Whatif? Howdidit? Where? Where?

Shush.

Then:

Whatifyouleaveus?

The mother always comes back, says Mama. You move
deep inside her then, beneath my hand your small back is
smooth like a husk, turning away. I ask:

What will we offer her?

Mama says:

Please please stop with that.

All right.

When we are together, we quiet. We fit just so, all sharp
kneed-needing.

jude

Sometimes when I look at them it frightens me, how little of myself I see in their faces.

I suppose it is not the ghost of the boy-father so easily loved and fallen, but my own gone girlhood that frightens me.

the first day

jude

In the morning they come out as per usual.

Sweaty. Cotton-kissed. Sleep has wiped them clean. They are dried dreams crusted in lashes. Summer sunburn, tight along noses. They are rumpled blonde-black hair, hug-warm. They are demonstrating to Harold the yellow canary how to sing. He doesn't get it. On the table are two bowls two spoons milk carton and cereal box, they are filling mouths with cinnamon crunch and V says: Chewwithyourmouth-closed? and Evan says: OK. They are reading the back of the cereal box like this morning is any other morning, stretched slow and fat and free in front of us, when the knowing enters the kitchen. Two spoons, set down.

We forgot.

Yeah. Yeah, I know.

virginia

We got to go to town. We got to take the bus to get there. The bus stop is at the end of the dirt road. It is two green benches separated by a wall of plastic. On either side of the plastic, people wait. Across the road a grove of aspen stand white and tremble-hot in the sun. Aspen are all connected, so they are talking to each other under the ground where no one can see.

I pretend that Evan and I can do this too. I tell him: I hate waiting.

He tells me back: No choice.

Fuckit. Sometimes I swear in my head. For a while I did it out loud but Mama said, Keep it classy, Virginia. Now I keep it classy on the outside but on the inside I say what I want. I hate waiting. Waiting is what poor people do—for buses in lines at school at everywhere.

Evan aspen-thinks at me: Elsewhere. And goes to the other side of the plastic. He's always doing that—taking himself under or on top of something. Somewhere else so he can dream. Now he starts reading the words scratched into the plastic: Need to get high call Johnny 897-937-9288. Rhonda K sucks—

Evan, says Mama.

OK, I won't say that word, Mama, but this one is nice: I did so love Jeni P, truly.

Did? I ask.

One of the girls with a cleaning bucket is eating a Jolly Rancher. I stare at her very hard and for a very long time until she laughs with her white teeth and rummages in her purse and tosses me a green apple. She looks at Evan, who shakes his head *no thanks*, and she tosses a second one, strawberry. Which he gives to me, so I suck on two at once, green apple and strawberry together.

jude

Airport workers. Hospital workers. Three cleaning girls speaking Spanish, their buckets filled with chemicals and paper towel rolls set by their feet. Their thick, dark hair shines in the sun. What am I going to do? Virginia smiles at them all with a brightness that eclipses everything. I never expected the voltage of this love. The world doesn't care. Keeps grinding its gears. From the other side of the partition:

I got to get me some sleep. Worked a double.
When don't she be working?
Minding her kids.
Electric's out at home—he forgot to pay the bill.
Working doubles.
Some shut-eye while I can . . .

No gas. How'm I supposed to get to work no gas
money?
I'm up early with the baby.

Inside the plastic wall separating the benches is an advertisement for the train. The train is from the olden days and
open-sided, coal-driven. It drags its own plume of smoke into
the mountains and tourists pay the big bucks to ride in its
bright boxes. In the picture they smile out of the open cars
and wave awe-inspired at trees.

You ever been on a train like that?
No and most likely never will.
Cost a lot of coin to sit there be bored to tears.
I want to see.
Someday maybe.
Maybe someday you want to throw that paycheck
down the toilet?
Be my guest, you can go walk up in those mountains
anytime. Don't need a train to see 'em.
They right there.
Rad ink, man—

The boy wears very big headphones, the kind that say *Don't
talk to me*, and yet he moves them off one ear to say this to
me. Thanks, I say, and he nods, replaces the silence, and I go
invisible again.

evan

You will learn your mother's ink: on her lower back float bus stops and butterflies. In the shadows between two ribs a child kicks a dog. Beneath the blade of her right shoulder a soldier crouches beside a shopping cart, his arms covered in doves. Two front wheels of the cart peel from the ground—the doves lift the cart and the man! Dangling from a rib glows a crumbling moon, also a feathered hand reaches down, down to the floor of that city, where an old, old man kisses an old woman very gently on her head. Two women fight over a loaf of bread—or are they tearing it to share? A tree, all leaf-blown. A girl bursts up and out of the dirt like a flower. The girl is V. Through roots falls a boy who looks like a bird. The boy is me.

A man she loved made most of them. She told us: That was a long time ago. He was very sad. He made the pictures with the sad, which is useful.

virginia

A little while ago she took me with her to get a new picture—there are so many pictures they grow into each other. We went down blind alleys and right into the beat-drum heart of the city to an apartment building the color of a dirty cloud. Laundry dripped from fire escapes. I galloped up the stairs, which smelled of pee, and Mama caught up slow with her big belly.

The woman who answered the door was called Jacoby and wore a navy sweatshirt that hung to her knees. Her nose was pierced. She looked Mexican or Indian or both.

She looked at Mama and crossed her arms and said, Uh-uh. No way.

Please, said Mama.

Too pregnant.

It won't hurt the baby.

The woman sighed. I don't know, she said. What if you go into labor in my kitchen.

Mama laughed. Please.

She had Mama sit at her kitchen table and they talked. She drew what they talked about, making a picture of Mama's words. And then she soaped up her hands until the whole kitchen smelled of Dove and laid out needles and ink on a clean white towel. She told me: Go on, sit in that other room and watch the TV.

I sat with the woman's little girl, who had the same large jewel eyes as the mama, and we watched TV. The little girl begged a sippy cup of milk.

Don't spill on the couch, it'll stink.

The girl came back and spilled. We sat there in a big, warm, wet patch of milk. When Mama was done, she called to me.

She was sitting at the table and the woman held her hand.

All right?

Just dizzy, a little bit.

The four of us girls waited for Mama's world to stop spinning.

All right, she said, and stood.

She was stripped down naked to her waist and stood with her back to the mirror, looking over her shoulder at the new one. I tucked myself to her side. The woman said something in Spanish about doors and daughters.

What did she say?

Every time a mother opens a door, her daughter is there.

There are four antelope twisting and flying up her hip, her side. The man at the bus stop can't see them because they are hidden under her T-shirt, but I can, if I close my eyes: they are black and white and amber and horned, flying there together.

I don't know the baby's name yet.

jude

E van. Get over here where I can see you.

Virginia looks up at me and suddenly I am a child again, a child inside another morning, another town, waiting for another bus, and that child's face, my own, looks up at my mother: *I'm cold, Mama.* My mother unzips her coat and I place my hands inside her jacket. I remember the feel of that now, my fingers tracking my mother's ribcage: two cold clasped wings. *Where will we go, Mama?* And I remember her face, her turning away. *No, really, where?*

She think you stole her jewelry.
I know she think that. I tell her, why I want those
ugly-ass earrings?
You done *told* her that?

Well. In my head I did.
If you ever see Jeni P return, tell her—

The poetry of poverty. The three cleaning ladies set their buckets in a row and jut their hips, resting slack-legged. The boy with the headphones cracks two knuckles and nestles the headphones more tightly over his ears.

Evan Woods, I say.

And he places his small hand on the almost-opaque plastic, so I can see it—not the child himself but the small shadow of the open hand—and Virginia looks thoughtfully up from our side and then throws her own hand up to meet her brother's. *Thwap.* And then, in one silent rushing moment, my children turn the slaps into a game, one twin throwing a hand up to make themselves visible and the other seeking it on the other side of the wall, back and forth, the mystery about where the hand will land, and how fast the other will find, follow, and join it, and I become breathless, all of us do, the housekeepers and air traffic controllers and nurses, all of us watch as the game speeds up, as my children go faster and faster, finding each other over and over again, the sound of their hands *thwap-thwap-thwap—* I love you! Virginia shouts. I love you! And I know she means all of us, all of us standing there.

Here is the bus.

Howdy, John. Work good out there at the airport?

Slow, I expect.

The damn virus.

Hospital busy?

Hospital always busy, man. It's a public hospital.

Damn dog got loose. Can't find him anywhere. You by any chance seen my dog?

Mick, she's climbed onto a bus before.

This to the driver, who has risen from his seat to come down and offer his hand:

Thanks, but I got it.

That baby not blessed us yet?

Soon.

Lemme help, child. I'm going to sit down all goddamn afternoon and night anyway.

I'm good.

Suit yourself, my dear. How're my two savages?

The twins bare their teeth and make claws of their hands, and the driver roars with pretend fear and laughter.

I lead them to the very back of the bus and clench my purse and watch out the window while the road rushes away backward.

evan

You got to go twenty-six steps down to the social services office. Thirteen if you skip every other in hops, thirteen down to social services, which is also the courthouse and gets darker every step, cinder block, chop-chop, walls yes, windows no. Then once you finish with the steps you stand in a line (*You two empty your pockets?*) and Mama, she puts her purse on the moving belt. Through the metal detector it goes. We lift our arms and stand on white-painted feet bigger than our feet while the machine whirls around us. And every single time we come here V forgets something in her pocket.

This time it is a Swiss Army knife.

So then you wait for V until everyone goes through all organized with their empty pockets and their purses and wallets on the belt x-rayed by the little screen and finally they pull my sister and Mama aside so they can check her.

Hey, Pockets, says the man who works the machine.

Mama rolls her eyes. The man puts the little knife in the plastic dog-bowl thing for her to pick up on our way out.

You needa wear a mask in here, Miss Woods. Sorry 'bout that.

And Mama takes three masks from the basket by the door to the next office and tucks straps behind our ears.

Then you go down the ramp lined on either side with beige cinder block and down the hallway with little see-through plastic bins hanging on the walls that hold fliers. And food stamp information. And birth control information. And now you are in the actual line, which is all built of women and children and always has been.

All of us, the whole line, wait for the three women in glass cubicles. They are the tired angels who will save you.

Once in an art book I saw angels on a bridge carved in stone, with hunched backs and looking faces.

Mama holds each of our faces:

Be good. Be still. This is important.

Then sets us up in the metal chairs against the cinder block, leaves us, and goes to her place.

V tilts her chair back on two legs, so it scrapes the wall.

Quit, I say.

I'm *hungry*.

Eat something, I say.

Like what?

Your arm.

We wait.

Want to play End of the World? I say. The rules are you can bring one thing when you escape. It has to fit in a pocket. We used to play a lot. We would run around wherever we were living, shouting what we would bring. CRAYONS, I said. A KNIFE, said V. *THE LITTLE PRINCE*, I said, which is tied with *The Tin Soldier* and *Where the Wild Things Are* as the best book ever written. ROPE, said Virginia. The game can go on for a long time. SEA GLASS. A ZIPPO. One time we were going and going—STRING. CHALK. A RED SKITTLE. KITES. CINNAMON—when V screamed, A DAD. The kitchen went silent.

That doesn't fit in a pocket, Mama said.

Now she's finally reached the front of the line. The clock ticks twelve and the woman behind glass slides a notice into her tray: CLOSED FOR LUNCH UNTIL . . . , with a little clock that says 1:00.

Jesus H, says a woman. And all the saints.

She is patient, though; she shifts her baby to the opposite hip. They are all patient. Our sister moans in the slow boredom and falls from her chair to lie across the floor, her hair bright against concrete. She wears her mask on top of her head like a miniature hat.

I use mine as a blindfold so I can't see her.

Co-RONA, whispers Virginia to the fluorescent lights. Corona coronavirus. Co-VID.

I don't know if she's asking for it or just likes the way the words sound: elegant and dirty.

McDonalds, Mama says. She's left the line to take us to lunch. We'll eat at the park across the street. Go on, I'm going to use the restroom. Wait in the lobby.

In the lobby there is a glass display case near the door with a little white panel that says: RESTORATION PROJECT: RIVERSIDE AFFORDABLE HOMES.

It is a neighborhood in miniature. There is our same long valley and river with trees dotted here and there, not too close together but not too far apart either, and little houses with miniature glass windows and porches with real lights that light up. Tiny glass windows and toothpick-sized streetlights glow over tiny paved streets and doors that open and close.

That looks like real water, says V.

It does. Perfect yards slope green down to the river, which somehow looks changeable and real, even down to the little stones at the bottom. And that is when I get the idea. About what we might offer you.

V.

What?

Pick one.

We do. Like Gods. Virginia uses the edge of her knife to pry it up, and I hide it beneath my shirt.

virginia

I feel bad after. Because Evan will probably end up in jail.
Mama, she sits in the grass by the pond where the geese
which are wild but not wild are sailing the muck and shitting
everywhere. I set out in the grass our yellow-paper-wrapped
burgers, cartons of fries, and ketchup packets. I unwrap a
burger and set it on her lap.

Here.

She doesn't touch it. Sometimes the baby makes her
not want to eat.

Want me to take off the lid, Mama?

She nods. I take off the bun and crisscross her French
fries on the meat patty. A vehicle for ketchup, right, Mama?

Right.

I squeeze.

Put the lid on, Evan.

Evan puts the lid on.

I'm starving, she says. She takes a bite. So do we. Fat, salt. Good?

Delicious, we all agree.

We all eat. We lie on our backs in the grass and the baby dances inside Mama and Evan traces the flight of a far-above plane with his finger.

I wonder where they're going.

We better get back. It's almost one.

Next, says a tinny voice through the microphone. What happens next is the Jesus H woman in the very front looks all the long way back to my mama and says: Your turn.

No, it's all right.

You hear me now, says the woman. Go on and get up here in the front of this line before you have that baby on the floor of this office.

My mama, she passes to the front. These women are queens, and I will grow up and be like them.

jude

You have Medicaid. They'll insure the birth. That'll almost certainly be covered. Food assistance I can do. WIC, SNAP.

SNAP?

Supplemental nutrition for children. Your milk, your eggs, and your bread.

Thank you, but—

You have a job? The income— You're living off tips, I assume?

I was. But they closed. The restaurant did.

The pandemic.

Yes.

How were you going to take care of the baby and work?

I hadn't gotten that far.

Let me pull your file. Birthdate? Those two yours?

Yes.

How old?

Nine. Twins.

Not identical.

No.

Tap-tap on the keyboard. Pushing with both heels, she rockets her chair back to a filing cabinet and removes a folder.

I'm sorry, Miss Woods. But it's showing here you're just over the income limit. I mean just barely over. It says here we sent a notice.

I don't have an income.

According to this, you haven't documented that change. Did you? Document the change?

I didn't document anything. I didn't know I had to.

Is your primary residence still 1415 East Second, apartment four? That's the address we have on file.

I'm in the trailer park. Island Oasis.

The father?

No.

Removing her glasses and polishing them on her shirt, the social worker exposes a strip of pale stomach, perhaps looking at the long, long line of women and children, children holding on to their mothers' thighs, women shifting their weight and shouldering the weight of children and those children laying their cheeks on the tired shoulders of their mothers; there are more piling up in the line on the ramp, a current of women that washes up every day to this window, asking for deliverance, and I know that we are not special and she cannot save us.

Which I knew before. If I'm honest.

They don't evict for quite some time, Miss Woods. Were you to stop paying, the rent would accrue. That's Covid protocol.

It did accrue.

CorONAvirus, says Virginia.

And I place both hands on the aluminum of the tray between us and let my hair fall over my shoulder and face so my children will not see me beg.

evan

Our mother's hair is thick and black and glossy. Her cheeks bloom. She has little red starbursts under her eyes from throwing up with the baby. You make her very pretty.

The rent. It must be a rather serious lapse, says the social worker.

It is.

Her hair is a tent. It is the night. It is the underwing of a bird and I want to hide in it.

You'll have to fill this out. I'm sorry—you'll have to get back in line. The woman pushes paperwork into the metal tray.

Next.

The line sways and breathes. From here all we see is legs. The hidden house under my shirt has sharp edges. I like how it is leaving a mark.

Evan. What are they all doing in that long, long line?

Waiting.

For what waiting?

I don't know. Papers?

I hate papers, V says darkly. Everyone here is afraid of something.

What are you afraid of?

They'll take us away.

I tell my sister, Pretend.

Pretend that below the counter there's a secret chute goes down. To a whole other world of basements. All secret underground basement worlds connected by doors between. And down there are lots of trolls sitting at desks in the biggest rooms you've ever seen. And there's our papers, floating down, swinging back and forth and back. Landing all over troll desks and on the floor all around. And they're piling up in stacks taller than Mount Everest and still more papers swinging down like snow. AND! If we are very very patient and very very quiet, our own personal troll will snatch our papers out of the air. If we are the most quiet and the most patient then we won't anger the trolls and then we'll get the stamp. And we'll win the game and then we'll get to leave.

I tell her, Right?

Sure, she says. Right.

Don't cry.

Fuckers, she says, softly, violently. Those fuckers.

I touch the house under my shirt. I can just feel the peak of the roof.

virginia

After it is done, we lead our brokenhearted mama up the stairs. She has to stop halfway up to lean against the railing because she is so pregnant.

Above, the world makes its normal world-noise. A car goes by. A person chats on the phone. Evan looks for a plane but there isn't any.

But at the top it's better. At least we're not underground. Or waiting. I like to stand at the railing of the bridge, which has a sidewalk running down each side of the train tracks, and I like to watch the water crashing below. I like how fast it goes without trying. It knows where to go. Evan likes being up, the higher the better, and I like when the train passes, how it stains the air with coal smoke and fills it with clatter; I like a noise so big inside my chest. Also I like the teenagers cluttered there, who don't wait for anything; they are ready to bridge-jump, smoking cigarettes and jacked up on energy drinks, half-naked, with their bodies warm and rounded out of their clothes, all skin and crackling heat. They touch each other. Against the railing. They touch with body and hand and open mouth. The river below is cold and clustered. A boy climbs the railing, an exclamation point against the sky. His body screams: Here! I! Am! He balances on the balls of his feet and leaps, the air doesn't catch him, he snaps his body straight and when he slices water there isn't even a splash.

There are long seconds where he is just gone.

He'll be washed away! Mama!

Then his head bobs up downstream and the others cheer.

He'll get taken to an eddy. There's one right across. Watch. See how he kicks his feet out in front? says Mama. See how he doesn't fight? She's right, the river carries him to a still place on the other side.

Then I see my brother's face.

You listen to me, Evan Woods, says Mama. That water down there? It's farther and colder and faster than it looks. That's too high. You land wrong, it's like concrete.

How do you know? he asks.

I know what it is to fall.

jude

A boy and a girl stand in front of Jake's Hardware discussing patio sets. The girl points at a deep couch and a glass table with a fire pit in the center.

I like this one with the umbrella.
OK.
Well. What do you think?
Whatever you want. Just pick one, I guess.
What about the red one?
They all look the same to me.
You could at least try. You don't even try.

The little bell dings on the door as the twins go in. They bend to pet the old terrier asleep by the cash registers. He keeps his whiskered head on his paws. Then they hurtle ahead of me down the aisle, by the hummingbird feeders and a teenage boy stocking bags of birdseed. Some of the seed has leaked and he smiles and apologizes. I pick out two rolls of packing tape and a fat black marker and load the flat boxes onto a pallet.

Howdy, says the owner. He works the register. Didn't you two tell me you was getting chicks this summer? He takes out a form and taps it with a thick finger. It's ordering time.

Then he sees the boxes on the pallet behind me.

Moving?

Yes.

He puts the form for the chicks beneath the counter again and rings up the boxes and the tape and the marker. Then he takes two bright lollipops from the stand beside the register. They are the big four-dollar kind with swirls. He gives one each to the kids. I dig in my pockets.

Uh-uh. On me, he says.

I can pay.

He pushes my money back across the counter.

Thank you, says Evan.

As we leave, the old dog lifts his head, whiskers trembling. Seizures, says the owner. He's getting old.

I have each kid carry boxes. Virginia wants the biggest ones, and she balances the flat cardboard on top of her head as we make our way down the road.

evan

Boxes! Split and sagged with tape. Stacked in the kitchen, the hallway, where does this one go? Everything SAVE or TRASH, nothing in between. Black permanent marker smells like heaven. Don't inhale that, you'll ruin your lungs. Towers of boxes. I love a box. Get down in it. Like you: huddled up inside Mama. Mama says: Get. Out. This is not a fort. Virginia! This is not a place for jumping off. Do not wear that box on your head, Virginia. Why? Because you will fall and break your neck. Sorrynotsorry. Don't sass. The day is almost gone, for God's sake, won't you please give me a hand? Get the other end of the couch. Out in the yard. The table is fine there. By the driveway. Doesn't matter. Mattress. End tables. Boxspringpillowsquilts. Everything. Now the little things. Candy necklace? TRASH. Crayons wax-bright with names like Goldenrod and Screamin' Green and Manatee?

TRASH. Glitter? TRASH. Save Harold. Something is wrong with Harold; he has no song. He is the Only Silent Canary. Toaster? Save.

Why?

So you can have toast in the new place.

Where? my sister asks. Where will we have toast?

jude

On the notice on our front door, it says:

TRUCK OR CURB

It is a choice. My father was an oilman, my mother an addict; she could piss through money, lots of it all at once. We moved all the time. He had a truck. It was a real beater, a jalopy, but it had a six-foot bed and when we left a place, we packed that truck like it was a puzzle.

I don't want to remember these things.

I do.

Night in the Bitterroots. I sleep in the cab, my father drives. A flash of headlights illuminates an arm, a bare foot, my father's cheek. We drive a high saddle between two mountain ranges, nothing for miles but sagebrush. Wide and open and unregulated land. Wake up, Jude. Will you just look at that:

the windshield a screen for stars. All these mountains holding us, sleeping giants.

What a life, he says.

The open box, set on the floor, with milk slopping in the jug. Cheerios. A rosary knocking back and forth hung from the rearview. My father's jaw, a hard line set in the dash light. In the memory we're listening to Nina Simone at top volume.

Dad?

The truck seems to pause in midair. Nina's voice stilled in a rasp. A flash of my father's knuckles, gripping the wheel tight; then all is motion: I smash off the dash, land stunned back beside the boxes. The engine hissing. Nina singing.

My father is talking to me. Somehow we are in the road, he's carried me into the splash of headlights. He is bare-chested and holding his shirt to my face. Oh, Jesus, he is saying. Jesus, Jude-girl.

What happened?

We hit something. Oh, God.

It's just a bloody nose, Dad.

He touches my ribs, my cheeks, my shoulders—Does this hurt? This? The milk has exploded inside the cab, on the inside of the windshield droplets of red flower on white.

Close your eyes, tilt your head back.

Blood runs down the back of my throat and we wait together for it to stop.

Finally, he says, All right. Think we're good now. He takes his shirt from my face.

Half in the grille of the truck, half in the road is the antelope.

Everything about that little doe was mad for flight, honeyed and white snow and black little horns curving into a heart. I kneel and put my hand to her neck.

Look at her eyelashes, I say. Like a girl's.

She's dead, Jude.

But she's still warm, I say.

I find my children on the kitchen floor each inside a medium-sized box, facing the same direction, as though they are in the process of sailing small cardboard ships across the linoleum and out the open door. There is a tiny model house on the kitchen table.

I pick it up. A white batten-board house with black trim, farmhouse-style, little windows and a red door with a real knocker on it the size of my pinkie nail. It fits in the palm of my hand.

Did you steal this?

No, lies Virginia.

Then why does it say—

Property of blah, she says. They have to say that.

Outside is the long shimmer that happens in June. Eventide. The screen door is open and so the dying light seeps into the kitchen; outside, swallows swim in violet air above the field and whip by golden-lit windows, take short, winged dives and gorge on shadflies. Most of the boxes in the kitchen are open or empty with long tongues of tape hanging, and in the cupboard above the sink I see the flowered paper I glued in so carefully beneath the juice glasses. Everywhere there is so much left to do. It's a new house, says Evan; it is Affordable. Maybe it's meant for us. To give the baby. And then he looks to me to see what dream I might crush next.

I get down with them on the floor, in my own large box. I touch the front of the little model with my pinkie, gently.

We might add a little porch, here. So we can sit over the river at night.

And here would go the kitchen table!

Together we stock the tiny house with imaginary furniture. We imagine food into cupboards and insert imaginary ice cubes in trays in the freezer and fold imaginary quilts at the foots of the beds. In line at the social services office, I told the social worker: I have nowhere to go. The fluorescent lights formed two glowing orbs on the lenses of her glasses.

The shelter, she said.

To bed, I say.

I turn off all the imaginary lights.

virginia

My brother asks: You sleeping?
Nope.
Well, what are you, then?
In between. I *hate* sleeping.
Why?
Makes you forget. Then you got to wake up in the morning and the bad has got to happen all over again.

V. Look. See how there is a crack in the ceiling of this trailer? If you follow the crack from the corner of the window to the edge of the trim, and all the way across into the next room and the next, you can see how the whole roof might crack open like an eggshell, let the night in. Imagine clouds over us.

evan

Below your window is a vent and that vent is supposed to let in cool air or something like a breeze but it doesn't because the only thing traveling through is a weeping sound. Whoever this Vent-Woman is, her crying comes out just like weather.

V gets down onto her knees in front of the vent and hisses: *Shut up shut up shut up.*

But the Vent-Woman keeps on like that, soft-sad hiccups and big-tremble breaths.

D'you think she's real? I ask.

Do you mean is she a ghost?

Yeah.

Too sad to be a ghost. She's real. I'll never sleep, says V. Never-ever.

We cup our hands around our mouths: Hallooo! Halll-looo, Vent-Woman! I try lowering things down to her. A piece of rose quartz, tied to yarn. It isn't long enough, so then we just drop stuff. *Chang-a-lang-lang.* A set of dice, rolled lucky double-six. Seeds. A whole cup of water. Crayon bits in all the colors. Nothing stops her, though; the Vent-Woman keeps right on crying, and I am wrong.

You can get used to it. It doesn't take long for the sound of a heart breaking to lull you to sleep.

Sometime later a silence wakes me. There is no crying, not anymore, and I am alone. V is gone. I think, No. In my heart I know she's been swallowed by the vent. I run to kneel and stare into it, into the dark vent, and it gapes black and monstrous and filled with echoes, leaking emptiness into the too-quiet room.

jude

C innamon toast. Want some? My daughter has arrived
on the step with toast.

Thank you.

Why were you crying?

I didn't mean to wake you.

That's all right.

I roll cinnamon on my tongue, thinking. Your brother.
Did I wake him, too?

He thinks it's someone else. Not you.

But you knew.

Yes.

There it is, on her face. The world's sadness. I set the
plate beside me. Will you tell him?

No. I don't think so.

I nod, and kiss her goodnight. As she goes, I think, There is no one pretends like Evan.

There is no one doesn't pretend like Virginia.

The baby moves inside me. The windows of the trailers float buttery in the field as men arrive home from twelve-hour shifts, from the garages and the kitchens, the oil rigs and ranches, as they drop stained clothing inside the doors of their homes to enter like kings, naked and tall. Children lie hushed on bellies in the blue light of televisions and women pluck hairs as though fighting back secret pelts. Through these thin walls trickle bedtime stories, lullabies, whisper-fights. The good smells of cooking. Frying pepper, meat and onion and macaroni. That amp of before-bed, running-through, slamming into. Someone gut-laughs. There is a stubbed-toe wail.

This.

All, all, all this to be taken.

the second day

virginia

I wake to the stink of smoke. Standing on the bed, I look outside, find a black column.

Evan. Wake up. They're burning them. The fields.

He opens his eyes and I see that thing in us matches the wind today. It is the white notice on the door it is the boxes it is the way our Mama is not out of bed. We let the screen door smack behind us.

Our hollering rockets us across the back field. We do not know the names of roads. Just land. The underneaths and on-tops, the places for climbing, for hiding. The sharp things that grow here: wild aloe, yucca, ocotillo claw and scratch our legs as we run. The ranchers are toy men, faraway in smoke.

I stand at the edge of the burning field and all inside me is crackling. Insects and mice dart at my feet, a squirming in the grass.

I'll race you, I say.

So long's you don't mind losing.

I won't lose.

We drag lines in the dirt with the toes of our sneakers. Allrightthengoalready!

Like flying.

Flying because you can't see the ground for the smoke. We run parallel to flames, legs split over char. Eyelash-crinkling heat. Fiery tongues lick the rubber soles of sneakers and I think they are hungry, these flames with their snapping red mouths! But little fire wants to be big, doesn't it? It is important to remember that big fire eats little fire no matter what. Swallowing smoke in poisonous gulps, we run, and the wind reaches up to meet us, the fire has tired of boundaries, the fire tires of being small, and the fire eats the field. Evan turns a corner ahead and his face is washed red like blood in a sink. All the life of the field startles and a flock of starlings flush holding the shape of the flames. Then the ranchers turn on the irrigation.

I stand there in the soak. Holdstill, says my brother, looking at the rainbows water makes, but I won't, can't, I am spinning round, arms out, water flying off me, the field hissing and stinking.

jude

Fretting of light around the shade. A darkness. I will not get up today.

evan

We come back into the park. Like we've been to war, my sister with an ash-painted face and grass stains in her white-blonde hair. Me football-blacking under the eyes. V stops in front of the Sleepless Man.

He makes your heart beat bold with the looking.

His body is still but thrums tight with watching. My sister's foot taps. Her arms cross. The Sleepless Man inhales and smoke fumes out, screening his face, and he stares at her with his terrifying black-bright eyes.

You hungry? he asks.

Yeah, she says.

He stands up and straightens his spine. Lemme go get us some ramen heated, then.

jude

H ere is a fairy tale:
Once upon a time the woman was a waitress in the
high plains. Snow was falling. She came out the back kitchen
door at closing time and a man was waiting there for her,
leaning against a rusted-out pickup truck in the parking lot.
Her hair filled with snowflakes.

The man opened the truck door like a gentleman. His
lashes prettier than hers but his hands rough from work—he
was a roustabout, a climber of the high oil platforms, and
maybe that's what she loved, at least temporarily, those hands
rough and seamed with the black blood of old dead things.
Maybe she could picture those hands on her from the start.
Or perhaps it was the practice he had of inserting himself like
a sliver into the sky. Most likely it was his body. A woman can
love a man for his body as much as a man can want a woman

65

for the same. Though it is rarely said. His wide shoulders and chest and narrow hips.

I'm too tired to fuck but you can take me home if you want, said the waitress.

Romantic, the roustabout noted.

I'm terrible company right now.

I don't mind that, he said.

The woman took off the black apron with the black book stuffed with the evening's tips and wrapped the strings around the book and set it on the seat beside her. She leaned her cheek against cold glass and when she woke, they were in the parking lot of the tenements, his fingers in her.

Mm.

He placed his fingers in her mouth. Hers was the taste of brine, also molasses.

The woman stripped herself of the button-up shirt and the bra, lace gone vintage with washings, and leaned back against the door while he pushed the black skirt up and over the hard fin of her hip. Halogen-spat streetlight lit the ink on her skin. The uniform all crumpled on the floor. He stopped and looked at his hands on either side of her ribs and said, Sorry. They're not dirty. It's just they get all stained with the work.

I don't mind.

Time went long and syrupy in the cab. Outside stood a single streetlight in the snow as though this might be Narnia instead of a tenement building and a parking lot full of old broken cars and apartments full of young broken people, and the woman climbed and climbed until she felt herself hungering to throw herself from that cliff.

Snow poured out of the streetlight.

I'm going to come.

Not yet.

The two of them balanced together at the top of something just perfect and then the man said, Sometimes I can't get the oil out. It drives me crazy. Then she bit the space between his shoulder and neck so hard that the next day there would be marks, and it was done.

Afterward the woman entered the apartment silently. Slipped off her own shoes beside the two smaller pairs by the door and stood absorbing the dreaming air of the place.

I remember the two of them on the couch that night. And I couldn't tell whose arm was whose, which leg; turning off the television, I knelt beside them both and put a hand to each of their chests and let myself feel the breathing. Snow falling like feathers gentle on the roof, and I should have known better, I should have been careful, but I didn't, I wasn't, and actually there is no limit to how many times you can make the same mistake.

evan

Much, much later I will ask how you were made. She will say you are a child of a little snow, and rust.

virginia

S et the Styrofoam cup on the ground, lick the spoon clean. Evan stares at our trailer across the way and I pick a scab on my ankle until it starts to bleed.

Don't hurt yourself, says the Sleepless Man.

She already did. That's just the scab, says Evan.

Cicadas clatter in the tree.

Can I ask you a question, Sleepless?

Depends.

On what?

If I can ask one back.

I think, then nod because I really do want to know. I been wondering, I say. There when we go to bed. There in the morning, when we get up. What's wrong with you, you can't sleep?

Well, my work. I'm an emergency responder. Not a good gig for sleeping.

You save people?!

Not really. Mostly paperwork.

But, Evan says, you're watching.

Sometimes, I think if I keep watch, I can keep bad things from happening. So I don't sleep. It's hard to explain.

There is a sadness adults sometimes carry with them like a suitcase and the Sleepless Man has it. The suitcase. He is just barely an adult, I think, like my mama. I think it was not long ago he was a child, and I wonder why he lives here, alone. I want to ask but we made a deal.

Why the gun? asks Evan.

What?

The gun.

There is a radio inside his trailer, and it squawks. It is a long announcement or something. It goes off and off. You need to go save somebody? I ask.

No. That's not my call.

Call?

Yeah, not mine. Some things are up to you, and some aren't, he says.

The gun? asks Evan.

My turn. Where's your old man at?

I look at my brother. Should we tell the Sleepless Man that we don't know where our father is? Should we tell him we never had any father at all? That we've had to make him up? When you are twins there are things you share only between yourselves, you can share an absence as easily as a presence. We have chosen which stories to keep, which ones to throw away. I look at the gun.

Maybe he's in jail, I say. He'll follow him there, to jail, Evan will. A teacher said that to me. Once.

She said that? the Sleepless Man says.

Boys do that. Follow their dads to jail.

Do you think that's true, then? About you? He looks hard at Evan. Evan shrugs loyally. The Sleepless Man doesn't say anything but he picks up the ramen cups and the spoons leaning neatly inside them and brings it all inside and chucks it under the sink.

Shit, we hear him say.

He's thrown away the spoons by accident. We hear him digging through the trash to fish them out.

Why'd you tell him that jail thing? asks Evan.

Across the way is our mother's window. Nothing moves in there. I go down into the yard and kick my heels up into a handstand. I'm working on my upside-down.

jude

A catalogue of left-behind places:

1. A tenement apartment. Drawn blinds with dim slats of light striping dishes in a sink. A spatula coated with dried pancake batter. We were hungry; we left an open bag of bread collapsed on the table, scrim of peanut butter on a knife.

2. A motel room with an outdoor corridor. The powdery bodies of dead moths at the doorstep. An unlikely claw-foot tub. I would sit on the closed lid of the toilet and crank the hot water all the way for their baths. We were pirates; we floated Tupperware into boats.

3. The country rental with blackberry bushes that left webs of scratch on small arms and legs. We were

jungle explorers; we abandoned mud boots on the floor, clots of dried clay on the carpet.

4. The freshly painted one where the last tenants had been unable to pack the kitchen table, so left it, full of pocks and scratches and dings, but the wood was real hardwood, strong and golden.

I unwrapped a pregnancy test and peed on the stick while the kids were still at school. Then waited at that table until I heard the bus, their voices, the tumble of them. Give of gravel beneath small feet. I threw the test with its two indicator lines in the trash and piled clean toilet paper over it. Picked up my phone and typed: Just took pregnancy test: positive. There was a fallen square of sunlight on the table. Then I pressed the backspace button until it was only a cursor blinking and went to meet the bus.

The places in which I am a good mother:

This is not a comprehensive list.

virginia

Where is your mother? asks the Sleepless Man.
In bed.
Why?
Don't worry. It's only sometimes.
Sometimes what?
Sometimes she can't.
Can't what?
Get out of bed. Heya, Sleepless?
What's that you call me?
Close your eyes.
I can't.

evan

L ook at our sister. She is really something.
　　Right now, the Sleepless Man is so sad. His wide-awake
eyes stare between his fingers. It is terrible, to not be able to
dream. To not rest. Then our sister comes from the cartwheeled
dirt of the red yard and climbs the stoop. She stands just below
the Sleepless Man. I want to show you how she places her
cool fingertips, with their bits of red grit, so gently to the
Sleepless Man's eyelids and closes them for him.

　　Heya, she says. Sleepless? You're good, Sleepless.

　　What? Stoppit, he says.

　　You are. Just tell yourself that: I'm good. I'm only tired.

　　You two kids better get home.

　　Say it.

　　Crazy kid.

　　Say it.

All right. I'm good.

One small tear squeezes out of his eye. I'm only tired, our sister repeats.

I'm only tired.

That's OK. V drops her hands. He opens his eyes.

Now the Sleepless Man and us, we are friends.

jude

When I was fifteen and the heat went out, I liked to ride the buses, liked to encase myself in the dark ribs of those warm and lumbering beasts that swam through the city. I could ride around the whole city for a dollar. I would sit right up front where the glass showcases the underbelly, the subterranean graffiti, those recognizable villains hunched in the stations, the homeless and hungry caked in misery. We got off at the same stop, he and I. I was pixie-cut, pierced. He was fragile in the way people are right before they shatter.

He pulled out a cigarette as offering. Inside the shadows of the hood his lips were perfect.

We walked together. He blew rings. I blew better ones through their centers.

Hey, catch me, I whispered. His ear cold against my lips. C'mon, catch me if you can. He chased me up, up fire escapes, hands quick, feet metal-clattering. Below us, rooftops floated in a haze. Tar paper flat and littered with old Natty Light cans and the scrunched elbows of cigarette butts. Pigeons sagged along telephone wires in feathered iridescence, and he watched me tightrope the narrow ledge between roof and abyss.

Careful, he said.

I took off my shirt.

Below, the street echoed with dusky voices. Unseen singers, a ballad of knockoffs, *Prrradda*, some hack purred, chanting: GEN-you-INE fo' *sho'*. Shakespeare in the park. The percussion of house music leaked out a window. It had only just been winter and I was pale and naked-smooth against that rough city. I wriggled from one leg of my jeans and hopped. He caught me as I jumped, and I wrapped my legs around his waist. A cadre of pigeons clapped skyward. The sky a bloodletting, striated with black tributaries of power lines.

I think I might be in love with you, he said.

Maybe he said that.

Not long ago, the virus visited trailer 567. Just over there. What happened first was this: It went quiet and dark. No one left and no one went in. Every day quieter, darker. Sometimes

I'd find the kids listening to the silence, silence interrupted by jagged coughing. People talked by the mailboxes:

> Someone oughta bring them to a doctor.
> They ain't got insurance, man.
> They ain't legal.
> They could show at the hospital anyways.
> True that. You get care no matter what at a public hospital.
> You going to show up there without papers, genius?
> All I'm saying is it ain't right.

Jagged coughing and the quiet and the dark and the sick opened its terrible mouth and maw and swallowed that trailer whole. The day the ambulance came, the old man my children call Yard Sale stepped out thin and pale and alone with his usually pressed guayabera all wrinkled in front, and they took the body of his wife away, a dried leaf under a white sheet. Why did no one come to save her? Virginia demanded, and I did not know what to say. There is that ream of light under the shade. Turn from it. Close my eyes. Perchance to dream. The baby is asleep. Maybe she has her thumb in her mouth. I don't know.

evan

Y ard Sale is asleep under his hat. It is late in the afternoon and the hot has sunk into the sidewalk. We walk by his plastic table piled with the folded clothes of his dead wife, then by the robin's-egg-blue car that never leaves the driveway.

YARD SALE
AS-IS: 1970 VOLKS
$200
runs
todo debe irse.

Every day someone from the park buys something from the table. Really no one needs those things. We need to buy them. We do this because, regret.

The sun burns. Maybe the world is on fire. We walk past 567, 568.

jude

There are two heartbeats in the bed. That is something to think about.

Once we were on the bus. In the seat in front of us sat a homeless man. He was yammering to himself. There must have been someone in his mind he was angry with. The man called the woman in his mind—I know it was a woman—he called her *cunt*. As the bus made stop after stop, he got angrier at the woman inside his head. He began to rant. *You go in you buy shit you don't need in the shops you look out at the hungry people in the street you don't care. You don't give me no pussy. You don't give me no nothin'.* As he raged, people got off the bus or moved to different, farther-away seats. The driver watched in his mirror but did not ask the man to get off.

Why don't you tell him to take a hike? somebody asked, as he himself pulled the cord, but the driver said:

It's the public bus system, man—a democratic institution.

I remember we stayed where we were. Evan and Virginia tight and small and watching. I remember I wanted them to see. The world's sadness is hard to understand.

I want them to try.

I want.

From where we sat that day, we could smell the man's dirty hair. The reality of him. We watched as the crazy ran through his body like electricity, the way he thrashed as he pulled the cord on the bus to signal a stop. The bus door opened in front of the homeless shelter, and the man angry with the woman in his mind shook his head—so hard!—as the bus stopped, he shook and trembled and clutched at his head with both hands like he'd squeeze the bad out. Then he went to stand in the line on the street, and we went to stand with him.

I was so tired that day. My legs did not feel like my own legs.

Do you have a bed for us? A shower?

We were given clean towels and beds in a dormitory.

The showers were like many others in those places. A concrete floor and white subway tile on the walls and plastic shower curtains. There in the steam a line of ten sinks and a long mirror. I bathed them, working my fingers through Virginia's hair, toweling, drying, and wrapping them.

I set them on the counters before the mirrors, said: Stay right here. My turn.

Don't leave.

Make me a drawing, a kingdom, I said. And then when I get out, you'll show me.

I stepped naked into the shower; the heat enveloped me all at once and I moaned with the pleasure of it as they perched on the counter and drew quick-fading pictures in the steam.

They drew me a kingdom.

I came out with clean, wet hair sticking to my back and looked at the two of them in the clean, white towels, the girl kneeling and drawing a dream the boy designs for her, a dream already fading on the mirror, and then they looked back at me and smiled. It had been a long, hard trip and still they smiled, I think to try to make me happy, and it hit me then, all the long miles behind and ahead and no money and no food and I felt for the first time it was all on me. It always would be, me and me alone, and the weight of those twin smiles broke something in me, and I sank to my knees and my hands hit the tile with a low, final sound.

They took them from me for a while, after that. Three weeks. When I got them back, they would not leave my side. Evan said:

You looked like you were an animal. Hit by a car, scrabbling in the road.

They told me later that it was Virginia went for help.

Virginia, when she runs, she just goes. You can't stop her, and you can't catch her because she was born to move that way, heart out in front. The baby in me rolls like a tide, and now there are knuckles scattershot on the door.

We're *hungry*. We're hungry, and it is your job to feed us!
Make something, says the door.
There's nothing to even *make*.
There's a ten and a five in my purse.
So what? So what?
Go to the store. Get whatever it is you want.

virginia

We look at each other. At the door that is doing nothing for us.

She doesn't like us to cross the highway by ourselves, I whisper.

Virginia. *Virginia.* Hey, don't.

I'm *not.*

I am, though. Crying.

evan

Highway twins at the edge. Cars rush by. I will remember to teach you to pay attention to roads.

You look that way, I'll look this. We go after this van.

My sister looks right; me, left.

Safe to cross?

Safe.

We hold hands. We run.

We are not mashed by a car.

In the Shop-N-Save we blink in all the brightness. It is good to have something to do. A way to help. We get a cart and take turns pushing and standing on the front, riding. Sometimes I push V and let go, so she can coast through the aisle, and people skitter out of the way and say things under their breath, probably like *Oh, I wish my kids would do the shopping*, but V and I, we are cruising by ten thousand kinds of sugar.

How are there so many kinds of sweetness?

My sister's hands are full of oranges. The smell of an orange is a happy smell. She puts the two oranges in the front of the cart, and one plops out on the ground.

That's where you put the baby, I tell her. That front part.

We contemplate this.

Where your mother at? asks the checkout clerk as we hand over the butter.

We'll take paper, not plastic, says V.

virginia

We did it. By ourselves. And now we need a rest. Outside the laundromat in large red cursive it says:

Betty's Sud's and Very Clean Dud's! Make's you Clean Inside and Out!

The chairs at Betty's are all connected, so when you move in one, another squeaks. I feel the sound in my teeth. Clothes swirl in soapy water and all around are good smells, dryer sheets and detergent and OxiClean. On the bulletin board by the office are fliers with tear-off phone numbers of people looking for work: Handyman. And also: Missing Cats. Who are not really missing but have been eaten by a mountain lion or coyote but their owners don't want to admit that and so are not giving up hope.

We set down the bags with the groceries. There is one machine going. Below the Missing Cats, a teenager spreads out across three of the plastic chairs. Her eyelashes are spidery with mascara and she wears a lot of chains—one weights her neck and one dangles from her belt, but inside all the black clothes and the metal she is small and neat. Her laundry is different. It pinwheels with brights. Suns, rainbows, and pink unicorns take turns pressing the glass. Baby and little-kid clothes. The washer is making the finished sound, all the rush winding down and the teenager wakes and rubs her eyes and transfers the bright things from wash to dry. A hot-air balloon printed on white cotton falls on the ground.

Why weren't you at school the last part? Evan asks, and I remember the girl's name is Scout.

I quit that fuckin' place.

Why?

I didn't like it. I want to be part of the real world.

I didn't know you could do that.

You can.

Those are pretty.

My little brothers' and sisters' stuff. They grow too fast. I use them to clean.

Clean what?

Houses. For rich people.

Scout pushes the coins in the slot. She's short one and rummages through her thousand pockets.

What are the people like?

I don't know. It's restoration. You don't see them, the owners. It all gets set up on the phone. The houses are all burnt or flooded to shit and they fix them up.

Where do they live?

California or someplace.

She pushes the last coin in the slot, slamming it home. The dryer kicks on. Evan asks:

Are those the houses down by the river?

Yeah. You seen the models, I bet. I saw 'em at the social services office, she says. Fire, flood. Once there's fire, the hillside can't hold the dirt, so mudslide too. They're super old. So different stuff. But it's cool—they got to keep the bones. That's the rule, with restoring a thing. It's like an old house—like a real old one—has got to be *restored*. You can't just scrape it. You got to strip it down. You got to include what's old in the new.

Evan asks:

No one lives there? They're in California?

Yeah. Someplace like that. Sometimes Texas. I don't know. It'll be people from somewhere else buy them. Idiots. It'll flood. Again. You can see the shadows where the water came up? There's like these marks on the walls? Like waves. The river come up sometimes. It just do. They'll buy 'em anyway. Those kinds of people got three houses, or more.

Wish I had three houses.

No kidding, ay? Y'all got evicted yesterday, huh?

Maybe we should go home, I say.

Not yet, says Evan. We might go live there, he tells Scout. At those new houses.

She smiles, says, Yeah. Sure. Maybe someday.

Outside it is the time of day when shadows lean heavy from the tree. We should go home. We should check on her. I don't want her to leave us. That happened only the one time when she got too sad at that shelter but I make sure it doesn't happen again. Tomorrow we need to leave. Sun going fast now. The big kids of the park come out when it gets dark, do big-kid things. Our shadows will look longer, taller, as we go back. But we don't go. Not yet. I can feel it in Evan, the thinking about the house, and it's there in me too, the dream of the neat little black-and-white boards, waiting for us, so we stay put in the red plastic chairs and we listen to the machine and its quiet whooshing and we stay a little too long.

Scout is telling us about something called demo.

These people, they go in, demo. Builders, but to be a builder you got to tear stuff down too. They strip whatever is rotten and broken away down to the studs and then build back onto the bones. Sometimes they find things. Like old shit, in the walls—whale oil, a newspaper article about a man walked on the moon. Wild shit. I go in on the back of the builders. Get rid of the bent nails. Sweep up the sawdust. Scrape stickers from the windows with a razor blade . . . I love it. I love the feel of an unfinished thing. At school they were always asking: *What do you want to be?* What am I supposed to say to that? I don't know. Do I have to know? Like I'm not already being something.

I know what we will offer, my brother says.

What?

To our baby, he says.

Scout doesn't look at him like he's weird. She says, Yeah. It's important to give a baby something. What I do is, I help them get dressed. My little sisters. It's a nice thing, dressing a baby. Fitting their little arms and legs into something. I mean. Look how happy those clothes are. Rainbows and ferris wheels.

We get to choose?

Not very long. You can't choose very long. Only for a little while. Until she chooses for herself.

evan

Because I am thinking about the beams of a new house, rooms that flow from one into the other. Because I am building the house, board by board, in my mind, and setting V free to run through the house, and Mama is turning to tell her to *holdstill!* in the kitchen, which is painted in pale cream, and because I am dreaming it up, asking Scout which way to go (*It's easy*, she says, *you follow the river, downstream not up*), and she is drawing it for us, on the back of a flier about a missing cat, and because Scout's drawing is unexpected—I mean it is interesting, small and blunt—and she wears all those silver rings and things, and because Virginia asks to wear the one with the skull, because of all this we stay in the laundromat too long, and when we go outside it is almost night, and we walk a little ways, and then by the tree there are voices:

Catch it, man.

I ain't going to. What if it claws me?
'S just a janky old street cat—
You catch it then, it's so easy.
Fine. Ouch—shit.
Fucker bit you?
Here's the rope.
Haul it up.
You want to go first?
This is kind of fucked up, man.
You scared?
I don't know about it is all I'm saying.
You don't want to, I'll go.

virginia

The cat twists on the end of the rope. The boys have hung it from the branch of the tree by two legs. Piss hot on my thighs. For now I stay rooted to this spot.

It is impossible to stay where I am, but also impossible to move into the place I must be next. The cat is a comma against the sky.

jude

The phone rings once then stops. Then begins again.
Beginning again.

Hello?

Miss Woods?

This is she.

This is your neighbor Betty—from Betty's Laundromat. It's your daughter.

Virginia?

Yes. She's been in a fight.

A fight?

You're going to need to come and get her.

I put one hand over the mouthpiece. Then take the hand away.

My son?

Yes, he's here too. There was a small group of them—I'm afraid children are not always kind. They were doing something to a cat. A stray. But she bit one of them and so I think you'd better come.

The cat?

No. Your daughter.

I'm on my way.

Thank you. And Miss Woods?

Yes.

Well, your daughter, she's wet herself. She'll need a change of clothes.

From outside I look in at the soft yellow light of the laundromat office: the kids are inside, their heads bent together, foreheads touching. I try to get to them, to open the door, but it is locked, and I find myself frantic, pulling.

Hello, Miss Woods.

Betty has very brown eyes and a wide body that makes you feel comfortable, and she begins to talk in a warm voice that sounds clean and breathless: You'll have to forgive me, Miss Woods, I have to lock up early, she says, nodding at the sign. If I don't, people sleep here—try to, anyway—and I'd let them, but I can't keep the business open and do that. It's a shame. Well, you'll want to know what happened to your daughter, dear thing. I'm afraid they put her in the trash can.

I'm sorry?

It seems . . . And here she sighs, as though she is tired. Come in, now. I don't know what they were doing. Cruelty. It isn't right and I'm sorry, but you know some of the kids around here are real shits. They don't mean to be, of course, but life is life is life.

She bit one of them?

There is a silence, then: I'm afraid so. Ma'am? If I may?

Yes.

I wonder if you're needing assistance of any kind.

I don't know what you mean.

I saw . . . I'm wondering . . . Do you have a place? Do you and the kids . . . Do you have enough to eat?

Yes.

That's good. Well, when I asked some questions, they brought up some things. Inadvertently. You understand. Children, they talk they know not what. Anyway, I wanted . . . I wanted to make sure you have a place. These two. Precious. I'm glad for a roof over their heads, glad for you. I'm so glad that's taken care of. Because Miss Woods?

Yes.

Your girl. She seems worried.

We are going to be all right, I say, but Betty claps her chapped hands together now.

Y'all's mama is here to get you!

And here they come. Looking up, looking out and earnest for me, they come, and Betty kisses them both on their heads and says, Don't forget y'all's groceries there by my chairs. Sleep tight, she says to Virginia. Sweet dreams, she says to Evan.

Thank you, Betty.

As the door closes behind us, the leaves of the cottonwood shimmer in dusk.

Virginia.

Mmm.

What happened?

I don't want to talk about it.

Show me.

It is Evan takes my hand and leads me around the side of the brick laundromat building to where the trash container lies on its side. Tumbled at our feet, a mountain of rank.

It's fine, Virginia says quietly, and I can smell garbage in her hair. I shouldn't have fought.

Let's go.

My daughter walks very quickly and I do not try to keep up. I watch her sharp little shoulder blades jutting through her T-shirt. Evan walks close to her. She turns to say something to him, and I see from the clean streaking on her cheeks that she has let herself cry. At the foot of the stoop she looks at me for the first time and I pick her up. I prop her against my hip and she puts her head on my shoulder like a much younger child, and I carry her up the steps and into the home that is so soon not to be ours anymore.

Tub.

All right, Mama.

I fill the tub with suds and sit on the floor beside her while she washes herself. I scoop up bubbles and place them on her wet blonde head like a hat. She does not laugh like she would have laughed yesterday or even this morning. There is a strange light in the bathroom that is the flicker of the bulb, that is not eating all day and being in bed.

Do you want privacy? It is Evan, at the door.

No, says Virginia.

Then there are three of us in the small bathroom.

Get in with me, Ev.

He climbs in, shorts and all.

You too, Mama.

I am enormous, I say. I don't think I'll fit.

You're perfect.

We'll overflow.

In.

All right.

I strip to bra and panties. We are all in.

Evan turns on the water and there is the sound of it rushing around us, warming. Our three sets of knees poke out of the water—Evan's square, hers scraped. My belly is an island.

Virginia's voice is clear and quiet like a piece of sunlight when she says: .

I was carrying the groceries by the wall and we were on our way home but we waited too long and some big boys were hurting a cat. Sweet kitty that likes the milk Evan puts out. We said, Please please stoppit, and the tall one said, Hey you. You two kicked out tomorrow—

And V said, No shit, Sherlock, says Evan.

Evan. Don't tell her that.

I don't care, I say. That doesn't matter. Go on.

Virginia says: Then the tall one put his arms on either side of me against the brick wall. Like this.

I nod. My daughter's arms are very small on either side of my face.

Like a prison, she says. And he said—

She stops and looks at Evan. He finishes:

He told V: Kiss me, Trailer Park. And V said, No, I don't want to. He said, I'll cut down your cat. And he did. He cut down the cat and said, Now my kiss. Then V said, I changed my mind. He said, You can't do that. I said, Yes she can.

Two held Evan. Virginia speaks in that clear, new voice. Held him. The tall one twisted my nipple. He called it that— a nipple twister. I said, I'll kill you. And then he tried, and then I bit him. He said: Trailer Park, I'll put you in the trash where you belong.

The shower curtain is very bunched, plain and ugly. I want to tear it down, slowly, with violence, watch each little metal ring pop open.

If we had a dad, he'd kill them for us, says Virginia.

Every family needs a fighter, I say.

Are you a fighter?

Yes.

But you weren't there.

No, I wasn't.

Virginia is looking for something in my face, so I am surprised when she says:

You can't always be. But I wanted to kill them, Mom.

Why didn't you? is what I want to say, because I want to kill them too.

evan

I touch, then. You. Tucked beneath Mama's inked vines and grasses. I want to borrow your gentleness.

Your heartbeat is under my hand when I hear Mama ask if the cat was OK. You know, she says, after.

V says nothing.

Mama nods. Says: I thought I was going to make this work. This time. I'm sorry.

I lean forward and put a bubble hat on V's head. On Mama's.

Then V says, quietly: The boy who did that has a hard life. I think he must.

The light of the bare bulb over the sink falls slantwise. It touches my sister's eyelashes, which are wet and clumped. Rap music is thumping in the trailer next door. It sounds like a large, beating heart. Virginia sucks a little of Mama's skin into her mouth. Um, Mama says. Are you eating me?

I am a boy and V is a girl and you, our baby, are not a fish.

The baby is a girl, I say.

Possibly.

She is.

Like me? V asks.

No one is like you, I tell her, which is true. Mama steps out and towels off. She is mostly bare and ripe. Says, I like myself pregnant. I like my body this way. It is powerful. I get out too, dripping in my shorts. I hold out the towel for my sister, and V touches Mama's reddened skin, the ink flying up like wind out of grass. What is this flower? she asks.

Mariposa.

What does that mean?

Butterfly lily.

Look how white. With all the black around the petals, she says.

I look away.

Now that I am almost ten, I am probably too old to see my mother/sister in the bath. You two, Mama says, come here. We are toweled warm-wet against her like seals. None of what

they said matters. Do you hear me? They don't matter. We'll
be all right.

Mama?

Mm.

What are these? V traces a silver stretchmark with a
finger.

Oh, that's you. And here— Evan. You see? You clawed
your way out.

virginia

Mama is tired; she has eaten nothing all day. She goes to lie down and Evan and me dump grocery bags onto the counter.

Flour. Sugar. Honey. Oranges. Butter.

I don't know where to start.

Where's the blasted brown sugar at?

Flour. Heeere.

This? Don't cut your damn fingers off.

Don't say *damn*.

Why?

Keep it classy.

Stop. I *know* how to use a knife.

'Course you do. Look like it. Nobody wants to eat your bloody finger-bits.

Chop that smaller. Like she does.

Use the rolling pin.

Can't find the pin.

Use that old bottle. The empty one. Here. No, rounder. Like that.

Like this?

Like that.

We are two twins on top of the counter. We kneel on the kitchen island, small knees, one black head bent, one gold. Our bumps of knees dusted in flour. Evan shapes the dough, a cloud. I punch it down. I set the pan on the stove to melt honey and butter. Evan uses a brush to spread melted butter on thick. Peels the orange. And I run around the kitchen island with the rind hanging from my mouth like a long tongue.

I didn't break any of the peeeel . . .

Evan is furious on his knees, furious with his fists, beating, blending, buttering; Evan says he is happy with the likeness. Happy with the arms, happy with the legs. We spread the brown sugar next, let it sink and melt in hot butter. Soupy sugar, then vanilla vanilla vanilla! The smell in the kitchen making it better, us better. Evan gasps: The egg! Don't forget the egg. Drizzzzle it on.

A giggle sneaks beneath the closed door and into our mama's room.

On the counter, Evan opens his mouth while I pour honey in. Dough twins, dusted in citrus, sugar. Layer it. Sweet . . .

Then bitter!

Stickiness in our hair. Peel beneath our nails. Flour thumbprints on foreheads.

We bring the bread out of the oven and study our handiwork.

Where?

The decision is unanimous. In bed. We stand in the lit doorway, the smells and light of the kitchen all behind us.

Mama, you hungry?

She is, just a little bit.

She stops when she sees. Is that a man? A man made of dough?

We know he is too sweet to be real. Bitter orange enough.

Are you all cleaned up? she asks.

Yes.

Forks on top of forks and spoons in spoons, says Evan.

It is eleven fifty-nine, I say. Happy almost moving day to us.

Happy almost, Mama says.

She pats the covers. It is all we need, we are there, solid beside her. The three of us eat the bread man, we eat our sadness. Is it a father? Is it one of the boys outside the laundromat? Is it a hero? I don't know. Mouthfuls of butter and brown sugar and orange peel. Outside and far away in the dark it begins to rain. A fine mist falling over the railroad bridge that crosses the river, the mountains. The train makes its long last night cry. Then the tracks go quiet and still in the rain. The rain fades things, smudges ground, air, and water into a pencil drawing. Across the field and across the river I might run and run, follow the river, turn, and disappear.

jude

Behind where the couch was are vines and birds, dragons and caves. There is a crow taller than city buildings, stalking away from where the end table once was. A map leads along the river and downstream and to a neighborhood of bright and lit-up houses in the darkness. Now that the furniture is out, crayoned drawings shout from all four walls. Vast, colorful explosions. I stand in the doorway of the bedroom watching them breathe.

I speak aloud to their sleeping faces:

It's the sweetness in you. It causes me pain.

They sleep on. The upper air in the room is that of children dreaming.

I mean, how you keep making good with nothing from me at all.

tonight

evan

We wake to the sound of breaking.
Mama?

She empties a tray of silverware out the window; silver hails onto gravel: forks, knives, and spoons. She turns—

Our pictures uncovered.

Are you mad?

Well, it depends.

On what?

Why did you make them?

Why not? V says.

We were sad, I say.

Our mama's eyes are a wild thing's eyes when she says, You made something with your sad. Keep doing that. I want rid of it, she tells us, all this little stuff, and she launches a coffee cup over the sagging stacks of cardboard, over the too-much-things, these things we never needed, the comfort things: the pillows, the blankets and books, things kept and saved because someday.

It's the middle of the night, V says.

Throw it out, she says. Throw it all out.

Lights pop on in nearby trailers.

Mama offers V a toaster, says: Make as much noise as you want.

Like a game? asks V.

Mama says, Sure, yes, a game.

V looks at me. Yes. A game, she says. And hurtles the toaster into the yard.

I stand on tiptoe to see. Like a beast, I say. With a tail.

It didn't break, V says.

Mama gives her a plate. It does break. And V's baby teeth flash, sharp and white in the dark. More, she says, soft and fierce. More.

We stalk from one side of the kitchen to the other, hurtling greasy Tupperware. Clattering mason-jars-as-glasses, old shoes. Farther! Farther! We try hard to outthrow, out-smash each other.

What next? What next?

All of it, she says.

All of it! All of it!

She fills our hands.

jude

Outside, the lights of the park blaze. It is done.

My children shed me like a husk, move on down the step, tiptoe on arched feet through glass and shatter. The light of other houses tosses a halo onto my boy's dark head and my girl's gold, as they touch things to say goodbye, pat-patting the sag-backed couch, as they tread between television and dust-shaded lamps and flit by sad-tongued winter boots, each cord a snare to catch their ankles, a ragged child-queen and her king wandering through alleys of the boxed and broken.

They're awake, Virginia says to her brother.

I know it.

The park watches. Neighbors stand sentinel on porches and in yards; they watch from between thumbed-apart blinds; there is the Sleepless Man, the old woman with a yard of roses who talks too much, the young soldier who has done three tours in Iraq and doesn't talk at all, and Virginia says something so quietly only I hear, and maybe actually it isn't her says it, maybe it is Evan, because sometimes words and children get all mixed up in the night.

I think we needed some of those things.

The night contracts and I am nothing, nothing but body, blooming, many-petaled, teeth clipping lip.

virginia

P orch light glitters on broken glass. Everyone sees us; here
I am, standing here in the middle of everything.
Still, no one comes.

jude

Falling to my knees in front of the toilet, I am wracked by spasm, bile. I wait for it to pass, then wipe my mouth and lean against the tub.

It stinks of 409, our ex-toilet.

I wash my face and hair with the water left in the pipes. In the mirror, my hair a long black rope dripping down my shirt, my stomach waxed into some pale, enormous moon. It's fine. It's not really begun. There's time. And yet. My body bows, knuckles whiten, clenching porcelain—

I check my phone. The contractions are ten minutes apart.

I will go to the hospital—I must, I must go to the hospital—*rupture, womb walls weak, tissue can split*. Betty's voice: *They brought up some things. Inadvertently. You understand.*

I have nowhere for us to go in the morning. If they find out there is no roof they will take them from me. I will not let them. Out to the kitchen. Just move through it. Here, open cupboards, grit on the linoleum; they are out there barefoot in the yard; I study their long-lashed listening.

The light in the kitchen goes livid and flickering; then it snaps off.

Mama?

That's the power, I tell them. They've shut it. Come in. Come on in out the dark before you cut your feet.

evan

Yard Sale answers the door dressed. Like he's ready to sit in front of his table again. One side of his hair is pressed flat to his head and the single porch light to the right of the door glows on his whiskers.

It's late, our mama says.

The old man nods. It is.

He takes a hat from a hook beside the door and puts it on. The hat sends a shadow slanting across his face.

Mama leaves marks with her nails in her own palm.

Something is wrong with her, whispers V.

How may I help?

Your shirt is dirty, V tells him, so he can go to Betty's and clean it.

Virginia. My mama pushes her back.

Used to be my wife, she would wash it and press it.

I am sorry. For your loss, our mama says, and then asks if he might consider selling us the Volkswagen.

Todo debe irse, he says.

Everything must go. The old man is awake now, moving by us, out into the yard, standing behind his table in the dark. He speaks his *t*'s with crispness: *Everyting must*. He gestures over the plastic foldout table with his wife's clothes placed neatly in piles and says, The car is the last. I will move back to my own country. Take a bus south. Some of the wet from his eyes falls onto his wife's clothes.

Do you have children?

I am not so blessed.

I have a hundred eight dollars, says Mama.

I do not need the car where I am going, the old man says. And he stands straighter. As is?

Sure.

And then our mother gives over the last of our money.

Everything is about to change.

virginia

Nothing changes. We have done this before. A car means leaving. What is different is that now I see it. This is some ancient pattern our mama is following, a pattern of leaving, of give-up-and-get-out, and we will go because we have no choice.

All of us.

The old man disappears inside his trailer and returns with a keychain. He gives it to our mama. Attached is a tin heart with wings.

He asks if she would like some of his dead wife's clothes.

No, thank you, she says.

The old man pats Evan on the head like he is a small dog, then bends down and whispers:

Tu mamá va a dar a luz.

I don't know what that means, I say.

It doesn't matter, Mama says, and folds over herself. Something is wrong.

Are you OK?

I'm fine, it's fine, Virginia, you grab what you absolutely need, no more—you hear me? Clothes, underwear. Water. A blanket. Water. Did I say that? And that jar of peanut butter. Everything is all hurry, all rush, so she doesn't notice Evan takes the tiny model of the house. That's fine. It is only small, after all.

jude

I hurtle us through the night. The two of them sprawl like puppies across the back seat. They whisper-tell a story.

This is the leaving part, Virginia is saying.

What? I ask.

Nevermind.

Then they are quiet, we all are, listening to the rush-away road.

Here, another contraction. I pull over and clench the wheel while it bears down on me. In the back they are silent and afraid, looking out at the dark fields on either side of the car. Mama?

It's all right. Shh.

Ahead the pinpoint lights of the little city. Gravel skids under the tires as I get back on the road. I hold the wheel with my knee and light a cigarette. Try to roll down the window but it won't go.

Your windows work back there?

No, says Virginia.

The fuse must be busted, I say. It's quiet for a minute, then Virginia says:

You shouldn't smoke.

I'm thinking.

The road to town is a long, straight shot. If I bring them into the hospital, there will be no one to watch them while I have the baby. If they are alone, people will ask questions. If a single word is spoken of the eviction, hinted at, they will take them from me.

We slide into the city and the sparkle of it blankets the car. Out the window the church spire and the pawn shop and the apartments and the laundromats and the OK Diner and the old appliance store that is only open on Thursdays. The small park with empty benches.

It's pretty, says Evan.

At night, says Virginia. When you can't see.

I turn west.

Where are we going?

Shh, I tell them. Go to sleep.

I'm not even tired, says Virginia.

Here is the small park-and-ride, a dirt lot. I turn there, then carry on over the train tracks at the back of the lot.

Where are we going?

I slide the car between long boom bars raised upward, like some kind of prayer.

WHERE? screams Virginia.

I told you I'm thinking!

IT'S NOT FAIR TO NOT TELL US.

I click off the headlights and press down on the gas. The car barrels forward down the straight road bisecting the fields and the rigs on either side and we are plunged inside the night and its darkness.

Stop! Mama! You're scaring us!

I hold the wheel hard and straight and lean back as the pale road rushes at the three of us. My children's faces white in the rearview.

I can see, I say. Calm down.

Veering into the field, I turn the car off.

The contraction that takes then leaves me wrung, wet and rag-like, over the wheel. Off in the field an oil rig makes its terrible sound, over and over. In the rearview I see the red glow of the EMERGENCY sign across the highway. I cannot believe how much what I am about to do hurts.

We're here, I say.

Where?

The contraction passes and we sit there like that, the three of us, looking at the risen moon. The milky light is suddenly everywhere; it illuminates each tender stalk of grass, shines on the hood of the car, it fills my chest. I turn to them.

I'm sorry I did that. Turned off the lights. I didn't mean to scare you.

I wasn't scared, says Virginia.

Evan says, quietly:

Are you dying?

No. I'm having the baby. I need you to listen to me. I have to ask you to do something. Something hard.

The night watches, white-hot and ragged.

evan

Y ou are coming. And we are not ready. I touch the house
under my shirt. I make a prayer for us.

virginia

Holdstill. You wait, she says. You do not leave the car.
You wait for morning time. In the morning, I will come
for you. Wait for me. If someone drives by, you duck. You
stay down. You do not tap on the window. You do not roll
the windows down more than this crack, here. Do not turn
on the headlights, the overheads, the radio. And you do not
come out before morning.

Mama all whimper. Knees drum-drumming.

Do you understand me?

I want to come, I say.

You can't. If you do, they will take you from me.

Tick tick, says the engine.

My mother says, You are my most perfect, truth-telling
twins. You are everything precious, everything perfect to me.
Do you understand?

What if you don't come back?
The mother always comes back. I told you that already.
I told you.

jude

Across. Down, down into this ditch, down on hands and knees, panting. Claw red earth.

When I come back to myself, red softens beneath my fingernails and I see chicory, foxtail, lit by the headlights of a single car passing. Taillights swallowed. The driver might think the red eyes in the ditch belong to a deer.

evan

A lone with each other, we each sit back against a door. We touch feet across the seat.

The inside of the car a steel cocoon. Rusted. The front windshield is so wide that it feels like the moon is in the car with us. Outside are round bales like ships passing in the night.

I hate waiting, says V.

There's a man in the moon.

That's made up, Evan.

No it's not. He's curled in that crater—see him?

No.

So I paint for my sister the outline of what is not there. See, I say: father-eyes, looking. There is his face. It's like ours. There is his hand, a knee, a foot. I paint for her a man of silence and reflected light. I make him up until he looks down over us in the car, fully formed. Then I take out the little model house and set it on the dash.

Are you ready to leave? the man in the moon whispers.

The peanut butter and knife in the back of the car say nothing. The cottonwood leaves down by the river shuttle their heart-shaped nothing. And water in the distance breathes in and out, says nothing.

It's too hot, says Virginia.

jude

The hospital is a world encased in glass. People inside stare into phones or at magazine articles or at their knees. A woman in scrubs sits behind the desk, her face illuminated by the computer screen. In one chair sits a man with a bandage over one eye stained by a brown blood splotch. In another a small child with a burned arm gasps as his mother stands, spilling him out of her lap, and then fits himself to her again, while she is engaged in a silent coughing fit. In the corner a TV flashes, a soundless episode of a food show: *Salt Fat Acid Heat*.

They should take the child back first, I think. Then the bandaged man.

I take another step and the glass door opens.

The smell in the ER is that of chlorine and waiting. Over the line of waiting room chairs hangs a sign that says:

I CARE. DO YOU CARE?

Yas? says the desk clerk.

I'm in labor.

You'll need to fill out this paperwork. Insurance informa-tion right there. At the top.

I have Medicaid.

The woman types something into the computer. Yas, we'll need a copy of the card.

They never sent one.

They never sent a card?

I shrug.

Didn't you call them?

I tried, but it was automated.

You should have told them you needed a card.

There was no one to tell. It was automated. They had me keep pressing numbers, but there was no one to talk to.

We're going to need insurance information to see you, ma'am.

Press four, I say. Or five.

Holding out a clipboard, the clerk says: Fill this out best you can, and I'll see what I can do.

May I use a pen, please?

The woman offers me a pen emblazoned with a phar-maceutical company logo: OXYCONTIN, it says on the barrel. EFFECTIVE RELIEF TAKES JUST TWO.

I sit and begin with the boxes.

—Two children

—Father: N/A

—History of Unhousedness.

Home-*less*-ness. I study the x's in their boxes and write a series of random numbers at the top of the form and then bring it back to the clerk.

The child, I think. Then the bandaged man, who is surely going to lose that eye. Then, please, me.

A home care aide marches in pushing an old woman in a wheelchair. She parks the chair and sets the brake, then goes to speak to the clerk at the desk.

I CARE. DO YOU CARE?

The old woman says quietly: It's my heart.

Quiet runs like a current through my body and I realize I have not had a contraction since the ditch. In the field across the road, I imagine the car half-buried in rapeseed.

virginia

I can't get this window down. The fucker is broken.

She said not to.

It's so hot.

V.

I slump back against the seat. Evan is up front. My head feels full of air, I say. I can't wait here in the hot. I'm going to die.

Climb up in front. Buckle up, Evan says, and I'll take us away.

This car is so old that in places, rust has disintegrated to lace. The field beneath the rusted floor is dark, and the sky above dark and ancient, so it seems the car floats inside sky, seems possible that if we ask, it might take flight. Oh, this car. We pretend it's ours, ours alone. My brother says, It'll take us anywhere, Evan is saying, however far. However far we want to go.

He wipes sweat from his eyes and puts one hand to the wheel and another on the shifter.

Close your eyes.

The car groans. Bits of sand and grass sift from wheel wells and float off, luminous. Beside him in the passenger's seat I laugh madly, we rise through a cluster of stars.

Evan? Evan, what . . .

We are cruising. My brother keeps both hands on the wheel. The car never hits a pothole, it soars, banks; Evan shifts and takes us over the hospital, the field with the round bales, the river, the bridge; he shifts again and we accelerate and fly between two towering cloudbanks, nothing beneath but great canyons of sky and nothing around but stars, and then somewhere in the distance headlights razor the night. My eyes flash open.

Evan!

The car jolts. The dream wilts, we return to earth.

A police cruiser whips by on the road, its lights whirling. I taste disappointment, sharp to the tongue. *You duck. You stay down . . . They will take*—outside is freedom, the sweet smell of hay, cereus like discs of powdered light—*You duck. You stay down.* Evan bends his head to mine and we stuff twin thumbs in our ears, we hum something quick and tuneless *lalalalalala.* We plug up our mother's warning—*They will take you from me*—and headlights pass over our bent backs, flash over each glow of eye, each muffled flutter of wing. When the police cruiser has gone and it is just us in the car, in the field, we sit up, and the first thing I see is the little house, on the dash.

The moonlight splashes through the tiny windows.

It's too hot, I say.

It's making me feel strange, says Evan. And he is right: the balloon feeling in my head is worse. I feel light, floaty. Evan tries again to crank down the driver's-side window.

It won't go more than this crack. I'll try them all again. He climbs in the back. There is sweat under my thighs sticking me to the vinyl of the seats.

None of them will go, V.

Night sounds enter the car. Cricket song.

V, let's go.

Where?

The night screams emptiness. That's the thing about leaving. You chuck things, the crayon stubs that aren't long or bright anymore, you crush the refrigerator picture, toss the photo without a frame; you leave things because it makes you lighter. And you might as well. Travel light. You might as well leave. Say goodbye to the good girl and the good boy you were, the ones that listened. We can grow into a new boy and new girl in the dark. Tougher, wilder, like seeds. The hot is in my chest and in my mouth.

V? Virginia?

I'm fine. I just went to sleep a minute.

We can go find those empty houses.

She'll be mad.

But we're making something. A home to give the baby. And it's so hot.

A slick of sweat on my brother's forehead. A droplet of it slides down by his ear. He closes his eyes.

Evan. Evan! Do you think she made a mistake? Leaving us here?

The mother always comes back. He looks at the house. But I can see it. Can't you, V? Can't you see it?

jude

The old woman seems made of wax. On the back of her wheelchair a piece of masking tape reads: DOROTHY.

I imagine myself years from now in this chair: JUDE.

Out the window, the traffic light washes the street red but there is nothing coming or going. The old woman looks at me with blue eyes, cataract-clouded.

DOROTHY! her care assistant shouts. YOU'RE AWAKE. CAN I GET YOU ANYTHING?

It's my heart, she tells me.

The care assistant hollers: THEY'LL BRING YOU TO A ROOM SOON.

I don't want a room. I want to go home.

The care assistant wears a nametag that says MAUDE. She rotates Dorothy's wheelchair to face the TV. THERE, THERE, she says, patting Dorothy on her crocheted shoulder.

Dorothy has a small white whorl at the crown of her head, like a nest.

They just get so used to their own environs! Maude is saying. You know how it is. With the old. Maude flops down. At home? She knows what to expect. ISN'T THAT RIGHT, DOT? DOT? At home we *know* where things are. How to put ourselves together. How the day will go. It's hard to leave, for the old. It confuses them so. And then, to top it off? Sometimes, many times, they come here and don't go home again.

I need to be home in the morning, Dorothy says. To water my roses.

She does have the most exquisite rose garden you've ever seen, says the caretaker. YOUR GARDEN IS TRULY REMARKABLE, DOT.

Ma'am? says the clerk.

That's me she wants again, says Maude. More paperwork, I expect. And as she bustles over to talk to the desk clerk, I see her scrubs are emblazoned with kittens knocking about balls of yarn.

She's confused, Maude is saying. She's a bit disoriented. I found her outside in the garden—she'd fallen.

A nurse kneels, and Maude places her own arthritic hand on Dorothy's ribcage, gently. Dorothy's bones are brittle. Her skin is thin and translucent and seems like it could tear, like rice paper; I think, There is very little division left between her body and the air, the earth.

WHAT IS YOUR NAME? WHAT DAY IS IT? WHAT CITY ARE YOU IN? WHAT YEAR? WHO IS PRESIDENT RIGHT NOW?

Dorothy looks confused and I think, This might be any hospital, any city in America.

The child floats inside me, flying through amniotic fluid, one tiny hand open, fingers loose.

I feel everything, you know, Dorothy says.

evan

When I do crack open the door and drop into the field, there is only a small sound—a cat landing. And then nothing.

My sister sits alone in the passenger's seat.

She wants to save mama so badly.

You have to save yourself first.

Inside the car, a slice of moon stripes her chest like a cut. The river breathes behind the parted black fingers of cottonwoods on the far side of the field. Cottonwoods mean river. Always. They shed seeds with tiny white umbrellas, like summer snow falling silently over the grass, the car.

Ready? I ask.

Things furred and toothed rummage through the dark. She is scared. But when she presses her fingertips to the window, I breathe clouds into them.

I'm afraid, Evan.
I'm going to catch you, I say.
We pour into warm dark.

jude

Dorothy is sleeping, chin tucked to chest, when all at once she wakes and looks down at her body like she's never seen herself before.

Sometimes, she says, while I sleep I am young. Then I wake in this body and think, not this old thing again. I will die at my home. Not here, in this hospital, in a waiting room. At home. Folding one hand over the other on her lap, she says: Well. You're going to have a baby.

Yes.

You're young. What is your name, child?

Jude.

That's good, Jude. Too young to be afraid.

I feel the vacuum left by the twins' neediness and volume and constant proximity, and I yearn for them, their compact bodies and their noise that banishes all other noise.

I remember holding my babies while they nursed, Dorothy says. I looked into their eyes that were the color of all babies' eyes—the place between blue and gray. Not special. Just mine. I looked and they looked back and straight into me. For hours and hours, we would look. There is nothing like it, that looking. No one sees you like your own child. She sighs. Your baby is a girl?

I don't know.

It is. It's hard to be a girl. No need to tell the child that. The world will tell her. Hold her while you can. One day you pick them up for the last time. I remember . . . Ach! You're good at listening, child. I'm sorry, rattling on, it's just—my mind runs.

It's OK.

When I was a child, I was very poor, you know. I spoke to hunger as if he were a person. I expect people think that's not the case now. Though they would be wrong. There are plenty of children in this world know hunger, his face. I like talking with you.

She takes my hand. It is not natural, sitting here, holding the hand of a strange woman in the ER in the middle of the night. But I don't mind.

Dorothy?

Yes, dear?

Where are your children, tonight?

The old woman closes her eyes. Opens—blue.

Strawberry ice cream, she says. That's the only thing I still taste. The taste buds go, when you are as old as I am. But strawberry ice cream. It's happening again. My heart. Please tell that woman over there, the one with the cats on her pajamas, that I would like some strawberry ice cream.

virginia

S wallow the night. With my feet. Every time I put a foot
down, joy. Like: Nobody. Can. Stop. Me. Scatter footsteps,
all the time river appearing, reappearing, behind bracken,
alongside the vacant lot, that mess of wire, posts, and metal.
We leave who we were behind. Breath hot, a fire in my throat.
I dart beneath stripes of reeds. Brittlebush and cattail knuckle
the banks. Down below the viaduct I slam to a stop at the river.

It yawns, stretches. It is a living, breathing thing, our river.
Always there, flooding or shrinking. We are not allowed in
the river this time of year. That is because it is June-fat and
roiling with mud. Wet monsters bob, snarls of root, riverteeth
rocket by.

Look, whispers Evan. And points up, up, at the railway
bridge, where a boy dances in the air, leaving long strips of
color.

It is a magic trick until I see the rope. He has tied himself to the railing far above and wears a harness, and the color is spray paint. When he finishes a color—red, white, blue—he drops the cans, and they *ping* far below to rocks.

He's making the tin soldier! I say. From the story. The one who fell in love by mistake. Look, the soldier has a gun like the Sleepless Man. The eyes follow you.

No. The soldier only looks for the ballerina, says Evan. I know what to do. We have to cross the river.

We can't cross here.

My brother rips foxtail grass out by the roots, and there is a soft tearing sound. He says: I wish Mama was here. She would know for sure—

Do you want to go back?

No.

It's not too late.

No. No, I don't want. Downstream, not up. I know that we got to cross.

And he walks into the water.

Evan!

He will drown. I understand that now. The roaring in my ears is real, a real warning, and this water is stronger than us. It isn't fair—I didn't agree to this. Stop, I say to the river. I am in the water, because I will not be separated from him, be left alone, waiting in the dark. I am up to my waist, water holding me, arms held out and ready. I want to go home, I

say. But I'm only speaking to myself; the water smacks my
legs and fountains up my waist, and the river doesn't care. I
call out to my brother again:

Evan!

Evan lets the water take him.

He is swallowed, like a toy.

jude

O n my wrist there is a small tattoo of a wing, escaping the white cuff of the button-down. It is Icarus, he is falling, his wings are intricate and you can see the pinion.

Recognize her?
Yep. Right. Waited on us once at the Ocotillo.
Is that right?
Do I ever misplace a face?
Before everything shut?
Yep.

Used to be I had to leave them for work. I taught them while I was at the restaurant to shut and dead bolt the door behind me and run the blinds down crooked on their strings. I let them turn on all the lights whether they were in a room or not.

At the restaurant my customers would ask: You go to college at all? Do you mind my asking?

No. I don't mind. No, I didn't go to college.

But you must've wanted to. I mean. You must have wanted not to end up waiting on people like us your whole damn life.

I would smile. Tap the pen on the edge of the table. Tell you wha. You pay for it, I'll go.

They would laugh.

It was only when it got dark that they were scared. There was a family that would fight in the apartment beside ours, and all night they had to listen to that family trying to kill each other. I told them about the man in the moon. I thought it might make the fear go if they could pretend someone was watching when I couldn't.

She was a good mama.
How you know that?
You just know. You can tell.

I taught them how to fill a saucepan with water from the tap and place it on the stove, then dump in a box of noodles.

I think you're supposed to wait for it to boil, I told Virginia. First, before you put in the noodles.

It won't make any difference.

She was right.

They will be all right, out there. They will wait for me. For us. I touch the baby inside me.

In those days, eventually I'd send my last table home and text:

omw

ok we wait up?

no. go to bed. it's late and school in the am

love you

I'd send emojis. Two blue hearts. i mean it, I'd type. to bed.

When I got back to the apartment, they'd be awake, and we'd sit at the kitchen table together, and I'd tell them all the things that happened while I was out, and they'd tell me. We'd share our small stories. We ate cold noodles. Watched episodes of *Woody Woodpecker*.

Don't forget your homework.

Evan would read and I would sign the paper when he finished his twenty minutes. Virginia never read but forged the same signature in the exact handwriting.

Virginia. You too.

Later.

I will know if you don't.

OK, Mama.

They'd ask me: Good night?

I'd say: Not bad.

evan

I look up. The tin soldier stands steady at the helm. I lift one foot off the silted bottom and the river takes me in its long throat.

The thing about a river is this: it knows what it wants. And it only wants one thing. There is only one way to go. It pulls me deep with a great force and I want to cry out, Mama! But I don't, because she isn't here. Water is. Water came down over granite and mountain and it was quiet once, a trickle, but all that time it was building and gathering and now it shatters itself against boulders, rushing toward what it wants; it is too big, the river's want, my kicks are nothing. It is like being alive. Silt in my nose. My body buoys up on a swell and then I am on my back and I remember to kick my feet out in front. I remember I need air. I fill myself with it. The water doesn't mean to teach you anything, but you learn just the same.

Then the panic in my body and brain switches off and my body goes quiet and waiting, waiting . . .

Like you wait.

All these long months and minutes you have been growing and waiting to enter the world. Listen to me: You trust when the push comes, you can go. You follow the water down. It will carry you through the great roaring and to a calm place.

Everything still. Everything hush. Everything dark, and patient.

jude

They've stopped, I say. I haven't felt any contractions for the longest time. Excuse me?

The clerk presses two more keys, *tick tick*, then looks at me, bored.

Yas? May I help you?

I've been waiting for hours.

Ma'am?

Been waiting for what seems like a very long time.

What's your name again?

Jude Woods.

Just a sec. She enters something, squints. Jude Woods, yas? It says here it's only been fifty minutes since you checked in. That's what the computer says.

The computer is wrong.

Oh, no. The computer is never wrong. And . . . typically, typically—

What? What is typical?

Typically, labor lasts a *very* long time.

Typically, people have babies in maternity wards. Then, to clarify, I add: Not in emergency waiting rooms.

Well, yas, that's true. The woman smiles a sympathetic smile that is not really sympathetic. But due to the virus. You understand. We are short-staffed and very full. And you say you have stopped contracting?

I try another tack: I like your nails.

The clerk says: Claws by Charlene.

Oh. Very nice. Have you had children?

The woman coughs. I realize the cough is her laugh.

No. Forgive me, but . . . Never wanted them.

Oh. Well. I can tell you, it's been more than an hour. And I have children alone waiting for me.

The clerk's eyes sharpen, her nails poised over the keyboard. Did you say alone? Do they have a responsible adult watching them? Ma'am, I can't allow information of neglect without making a mandatory report—

No, that's not what I meant, I say smoothly. Not alone, just without *me*.

Oh. Well, that's different. It shouldn't be long now. You understand. She gives me the stack of papers. I have a few more things I'll need you to fill out while you wait. Releases. So on and so forth.

I already did all that.

The alarms in the back are going crazy.

You'll need to excuse me, says the clerk. Can you fill this out?

The traffic light outside the hospital changes on the asphalt: green, yellow, red. Then, crossing the parking lot in slow, exhausted steps appears a boy. He heads for the entrance to the ER, carrying a girl in his arms.

virginia

I t carries us across and then the river changes, black-velvet and purring. A wet head cracks the surface gleaming, and it is my brother, and I make my body a blade, slice the eddy, surfacing and spouting, tunneling underwater. We play, we shred stars with dog-paddle hands. When we climb out, our clothes are stuck to us like old skins. We peel off T-shirt and shorts—wring them and hang them on ditch willow.

We sit on the muddy bank. Gooseflesh. Evan beside me, skinny in underwear. Our arms hug our knees.

I thought you were trying to kill us, Evan.

You should trust me more than that.

jude

A thing out of some strange fairy tale: the boy appearing out of asphalt, carrying a girl asleep? No, not asleep, sleeping is sleeping; this girl is unconscious, her head tipped back to reveal the heart-shaped underside of her jaw. Standing on the other side of the glass, the boy meets my eyes and people rush around him. They lift her from him, and then I don't see what happens next because the charge nurse takes my elbow and says:

Jude, the doctor will see you now.

They've stopped.

That happens sometimes. I'm going to place my hands here. You may feel a coolness. It's normal. He presses. Sometimes, when women get here, it happens like that. The contractions stop for a while and then come back all at once. Often with a ferocity. He smiles. There. Are you comfortable?

Yes.

My feet are cold in the steel stirrups. His fingers probe inside.

Twenty-five, the attending nurse says to the doctor. She adds: Third child.

On the ceiling, torn from some nature calendar, is a photograph. JUNE: a picture of wilderness, a young jaguar.

Breathe, the doctor says, that's it—I want you to breathe in very deeply—good. Release. Good. Definitely dilated, he says to the nurse. You'll have your baby tonight, Miss Woods. He smiles.

But they've stopped.

It's the shock of getting to the hospital. He wheels his chair back. Go ahead and sit up please. Do you mind? I'd like to talk.

I sit, holding the gown closed.

Miss Woods. Sometimes? If the hospital makes you uncomfortable, or nervous, it's like hitting the pause button. That's what this is; it's a pause. But then, suddenly, we're off to the races. So you've done the right thing, coming in. I see here on your chart you need a C-section. Tell me, Jude. When was the last time you saw a doctor?

A few months, maybe. My hair is cold against the skin of my back.

He looks at me steadily.

Maybe a little longer.

Miss Woods, you should have had regular checkups. Your chart says you haven't been seen. The insurance would have covered that.

We moved. I did do the telehealth in the last place.

Ah. Telehealth. Did you vaccinate?

I nod. Is the baby OK?

There's no reason to believe she's not. But you should have seen us every month, and recently, as you got closer, every week. This child should have been measured, he is saying, and I think, Of course. Because birth is like anything else: you can slot it, schedule it, put it on a calendar, and pick it up on the way home.

What do you do, Miss Woods? For work?

In the fluorescent light, the inner skin of my wrists is patterned with small, dark burn scars from hot plates. I say: I waitress. Not for a while now.

The pandemic.

Yes.

That would have been hard on waitresses. I hadn't thought about it, he says. I'm sorry about that. Where was it?

The Ocotillo.

Busy place, that.

The Ocotillo, for me, had been dead leaves skating the sidewalk. Neon red sign. Antelope taxidermy hanging on the walls, burnished glass eyes gleaming. Over the course of a night, tables would turn four or five times and the charge for drinks would be four or five times the charge for food. The chef, a man of hard consonants and red hair, always said: People don't come here for fancy. They're hungry. Fat, meat on the bone, salt. That's what these men want. You've got to understand the terroir of a place if you're going to sell.

Most of my customers were rig workers, I say.

Ah. I used to work in the trauma ward. There's a lot of injuries in that field. I saw a lot of them.

Men who came in blowing warm air on cold hands, their chins ducked against the wind. They'd have whiskey neat, thanks.

That seems like a long time ago now, I say.

Well, says the doctor. You are where you are now. Which is where you are supposed to be. Would you like to listen for your baby's heart?

Yes. But . . . I'm afraid.

Try the breathing, he says gently. Try that again. Now lean back, dear.

I breathe. It hurts, and it helps. The two things at once.

The nurse lets out petroleum jelly in a flatulent squirt. The doctor turns the switch on and the screen lights up and the ultrasound wand travels my tattooed abdomen, parting fields of foxtail, wild grasses, sheaves slendering up my swollen stomach, spreading and splitting, heavy with seedheads at my breasts. The ultrasound parts the grasses, and my inner nebula bursts forth and I search for the blurred constellation of the child. There: floating, tiny chin on fist.

Rodin's *Thinker*, the doctor says after a moment. Beautiful.

Yes.

The room is quiet. Maybe it's the baby's quiet, a hush before becoming.

Is everything OK? Why can't I hear her?

virginia

Tick-tick space. We drag ocotillo wands along a fence. A cloud blankets the moon.

Can't see.

Me either.

I hold my hand in front of my face and can't even see that. My hand is gone. Holdstill, my brother says. Wait.

I can't.

There is something massive in the dark. This field is alive.

V?

I smell the sharp stink of manure, a bite of juniper. This dark, I think, is horned.

Something thunders by in the blackness and my heart bursts free of its cage. The cloud glides on; everything lit.

We are inside the herd.

Furred, jagged-horned. They are longhorns—red and shaggy with night-wet eyes. Red haunch, a red shoulder. We slip through matted fur and muscle. Slow, says Evan. Go easy. There is a barbed-wire gleam in their eyes. Evan whispers: We become. One of them. I feel horns sprout from my forehead. Lungs like bellows. A beat-drum heart. One monster swings its massive head around and my brother starfishes a hand on the creature's forehead.

Smell *that*, I whisper.

Warm. And beasty. Holdstill.

No, I say.

I tell the bull: Your breath . . . smells like *grass*! And my scream spins loose over the field; we whoop, running, dodging, fingers pointing from our foreheads like horns, we bellow, we are let loose. The longhorns jolt their heads in the dark, spooked by us, our strange bodies bowing in the field. We hold wire wide for each other. I don't let Evan see me fall. Flesh ribbons from my knee, grit jams beneath skin, but then I'm up and running.

evan

Y ou can walk the lip of an arroyo. Sometimes inside the
canyon you find a hanging island, a miniature oasis, like
the canyon is cupping grass and tree in its palm. On the floor
of this one, a perfect skeleton.

Fell down, V says. Elk? Musta cried out and out and no
one came.

It would have had grass. Water. Everything it needed,
I say.

Trapped. Until one day it lay down and died.

Yes, I say. But then the sun came, and the leaves and
the wind. Polished its bones, and then the rains. Grass grew
up through the eye sockets and flowers between the ribs—

Evan?

Yeah.

Stop.

All right.

You always do that.

Do what?

Take something sad and make it beautiful. Don't. Not now.

Why?

Because I'm trying to think about what's real. I'm trying to grow up.

All right.

Never mind. You can't help it. Want to play a game?

Yeah.

We play moths.

We are doing this, flitting side by side, when we step without knowing onto some rancher's land, so busy playing the game we don't even notice we are on a wide lawn, dark, wet, and soft, our feet still and silent, until we see a window hanging on the night.

We are surrounded by little gnarly trees.

Night cherries, my sister says.

They are tiny black moons gleaming. We pass into the trees and fill our mouths with sweet.

They're still warm.

That sun was hot today.

The way light hits the black fruit makes me look at the house. I do not know about this light.

It makes me think of you.

Makes me think of that other light, the hospital kind, where our mother waits. Or sleeps? Will she split open like a milkweed pod? Will she spill white down? Does the light from the home I am taking us to fall out into the yard in the shape of a window?

jude

The wand glides over my slick stomach and the nurse fiddles with a switch on the machine. The baby floats but is silent. Heartbeat? the nurse asks.

One day not long ago, I took Virginia for a walk. What about Evan? she asked. Just us, I told her. We walked out into the field. We walked by fox dens. Why are there so many? She asked. Sometimes the fox, he will make a fake home so you don't really know where the babies are, I told her. We sat by the river and skipped rocks.

Mama. Do you think I'll be a good big sister?

It's hard to be a girl. Everyone and everything will tell you it's up to you to take care of things. Take care of people.

What if I don't want to?

You will. You will want to take care. But that doesn't mean you should. Not all the time.

Do you always want to take care of me?

Not all the time.

But you do.

Yes, but what I'm telling you is—

What are you telling me?

I can't protect you from the world.

Mama. I'm part of it.

One day not long ago, when I couldn't sleep, I woke Evan. We sat on the stoop together. Moths banged their bodies against porch light.

They're looking for the moon, I told him.

Don't worry, Mama. I'll be a good brother.

It's hard to be a boy. People will tell you that you can't cry. That's not true.

I cried just yesterday.

Why?

He told me about a bird that died. It hit the window, he said. Too hard. He told me how he buried it and covered the grave with the asters that grow in the ditches. And then how, in the bush, he found the nest filled with freckled eggs. He and I were quiet together.

What did you do with the eggs?

Put them in a shoebox. Under the bed.

Why didn't you tell me?

We're going to try to teach them how to be alive. Mama—What is it? Why are you crying?

You are the most beautiful boy I know.

They might have already died, he said frankly. Or they aren't born yet. It's a toss-up.

virginia

M e and Evan used to play dead.
What it looked like was this:

I stole chalk from school and found a spot on the sidewalk. We traced each other in different poses: elbows a-jut or
body splayed or spread-eagle or ball-crumpled. We made at
least twenty. Every dead chalk kid different. Then, after, we
climbed into the tree to see what happened when someone
came.

It was the Sleepless Man found them.

He came back from his work saving people. He got out
of his pickup and stood there in the middle of the street for
a very long time, looking. He turned very white, almost to
stone. Then he went and got a hose and a bucket and a big
sponge and washed the street. When he was done, he sat
down on his stoop.

I climbed down the tree to show him my cartwheel.

Watch me? I asked.

I'm watching, he said. But he looked sad.

I told Mama about it; she thought and looked at him, out on his stoop, and said, Maybe for him? Your game is too close to what is real.

Evan, I say now. We're lost. Aren't we, Evan?

We aren't lost.

Well, we aren't not lost.

jude

The fluorescent light in the hospital room flickers once, and there is silence, and the moment expands, the way dough does in warmth. I think of the boy who carried in the girl.

You never know when someone will be lost to you.

And I think of the car in the field. And the nurse says, Oh, honey, into this room that does not make the sound of a heartbeat, and I can't stand it at all, so I slap a hand to my own stomach.

Find her.

A heel—or is it a fist?—notches into my cupped palm. A pulse charging the room, insistent, demanding, and I grin wildly at the doctor.

Men, money, these things fall from my hands, but not children, no; children I can hold.

the small hours

the park sleeps

The locksmith begins his workday long before dawn. Some of the places he visits are far from the office. The first address is an apartment, unoccupied, on a side street. He sets his black bag of tools on the stoop. He removes the two visible bolts in the run assembly plate and pulls the dead bolt lock free. He uses the light on his phone. He can now see through the hole in the door: empty kitchen. He removes the two remaining screws and pulls the dead bolt out and installs the new one. UP is labeled. This makes it easy. Then he inserts the bar through the channel and positions the lock mechanism so the keyhole is vertically aligned.

He tests the knob.

It does not turn.

He puts the new key in his pocket for the landlord and goes and gets in his little pickup and checks his address book to go to the next place. The wind rushes in through the pickup.

Night in the desert and mountains. The pines still and quiet against the sky. Now the moon's a coin, in the river, moving, moving downstream over rock and stone. Pushing against the banks. Cicadas in the umbrellas of the trees, whirring. Their hundred-year sleep. Rubbing dirt from their legs to sing. The field quiet, dew-laden.

Over an hour north, the park sleeps. Windows cracked to let in the night. A child's foot escapes a quilt. Her mother tucks her in tighter. As soon as the parent leaves, the child pushes the quilt off again; it puddles on the floor. Small snores. The river slowly wearing down the banks. Night cups the park in the palm of its hand, all around, the deep clear darkness of June.

virginia

This forest is lit magic. There is a fallen tree; I balance-beam it.

Hey, Evan. Hey, look. Watch me go, I say, and point my toes all the way across.

V?

S'nothing.

What happened to your knee?

I told you, nothing.

Siddown.

Don't touch it, Evan. It hurts.

You got half the desert in there.

Don't.

Look up, look there.

The ceiling of the trees is thick with milk-light. It's too big, the roof of the world, so I look down. Leaf-shadow troubles the back of my brother's neck and his bare arms and my legs. I can't tell whose body is whose. Sprouted up through long grass beneath the tree are the blooms of arnica, poisonous-yellow bright.

Whadja *do*, anyways?

Slipped.

Why didn't you tell?

I don't know.

You could put arnica on it. Arnica everywhere. But don't eat it.

I wouldn't eat it. I'm not a ass.

If you eat it, you die.

He plucks a stone from my flesh.

Ouch. Don't. Evan?

What?

Do you ever think she just wants to leave us?

I don't know what you mean.

Us. Leave us. I mean it. Did she leave for good this time? Leave us in the car? Would we have sat there forever?

My brother's face is close to my ripped-up knee and his breath is warm. He peels back a flap of skin and says: Why would you say that?

She did once.

She didn't leave. They took us.

Sometimes, Evan? I'm afraid to say it, but I think it. I think it would be easier for her. Without us.

He is quiet before he says: It would.

That's not what you're supposed to say.

Sometimes, he says, I have this dream. In it, you and I, we're real high up. At the edge of something. It's dark below and all the lights of a city are beneath us and I look down and I have this one feathered hand.

Only one?

Yeah.

You can't fly with one.

There's one.

Oh.

Like, we're real high up. Tall as those trees.

Don't tell what happens next.

My brother leans over my leg and says quietly, All right. I won't.

Careful, Evan. Actually, please don't, I say, but my brother's mouth is warm as he sucks, spits. He's getting the dirt out so there will be no infection later. Blood runs in a clean rivulet down my leg to wet the bark of the tree. It looks black. Evan says: All right.

Arnica gleams bright in the grass. Like fallen stars.

Evan. It's weird, isn't it? How you can need a little poison. But not too much.

We slip down, winding through trees taller than any buildings we know. Somewhere water is running, but it is friendly water, not too fast or harsh. It is the water that feeds small growing things.

jude

A moment, please, Miss Woods—
The doctor's smile fades as quickly as her heartbeat as he listens. He cocks his head and says, Stress—stress
something something. The nurse types. He zooms in. There.
Curled quiet seahorse.

Do you see? he asks.

That's the heart, I say.

Yes. He counts the chambers, tapping the screen with
the butt of his pen—one, two, three, four—and I watch the
magic tissue open and close, flip-flutter butterfly heart.

Did you hear that? the doctor says. A skip. Just a little
pause.

I don't hear any skip.

Murmur? says the nurse.

We've got to get her admitted, he is saying. Stress.

I say, suddenly: I don't know if I'm ready—

He says, gently: Not that I think there's a choice, but may I ask why not?

I go silent. The list seems too big to get into.

Your baby's heart is under a little stress. Nothing to worry about—you're full-term—but what I'm saying is, it's almost time.

The nurse wipes my stomach with a paper towel and the doctor washes his hands at the small sink, turning to speak to me over his shoulder:

Sometimes, he says, babies are ready for the world before their mothers are ready to bring them into it. I'm going to have you up there in just a minute. You're going to go on and make yourself as comfortable as you can. I mean right away, and I'll get you a room in Maternity. Do you understand? Since the ward is full, I'll have you wait in the ER again, but it will be only for a moment. Not long. If you have another contraction, I want you to tell the charge nurse immediately. We'll have that room ready as quickly as possible. He stands, says under his breath to the nurse: I need a room. And Miss Woods?

Yes.

You're young. Strong. Tonight . . . I don't quite know how to say this. He works a dry paper towel between his fingers and looks at me directly. Tonight, you need to put this baby first. I don't know what it is, on your mind, but this baby is coming.

Then he goes, closing the door. On it hangs a paper towel dispenser with a sign: ALWAYS WASH YOUR HANDS BEFORE AND AFTER TOUCHING A PATIENT.

I sit up. The nurse's eyes latch on to my tattooed back, then slide off.

It's fine, I tell her. You can look. Really. That's what they're for.

When, the nurse says, aligning instruments on a clean towel, did you get them?

All different times.

I hear—the nurse places a metal clamp neatly on the counter—I hear it's like an addiction.

It's like that. Like they say.

Does it hurt? she asks.

Yes.

Then why?

Hurt. Followed by something beautiful.

I'll leave you to get dressed.

The door shuts, and I am alone. I slide off the table, the wet stain of me left on the paper.

The boy who carried the girl is in the waiting room. He seems to be wilting in his hospital chair. I imagine him surrounded. A white stamen in the center of black petals, folding open, drooping, fluttering to the ground. He is pale and delicate.

Sixteen, maybe a young seventeen. Every few minutes some monumental worry and corresponding pain seems to course through him and he closes his eyes to meet it in the dark.

He seems unsalvageable, even to me.

I want to get outside. To cross the road and peer into the windows of an old car at my sleeping children. I don't want to wake them or bring them here. I only want to place my palm on their chests and check, the way I did when they were infants, that they are breathing. In the morning I will tell them all about this boy that carried in the girl to be saved.

You're staring.

Sorry, I say.

You awright?

Fine.

He shoves his fists far down in the pockets of his jeans and leans his handsome dark head back against the wall and looks at me from beneath long lashes.

You don't look it, says the boy.

Thanks, I say. Not that it's your business anyway.

No, it's not. But I can tell a person in a hospital waiting room, someone knocked up like you, may be not all right. Waiting all alone. It don't take a genius to see that. None of my business, though, you're right.

I laugh out loud. He moves the toe of one black sneaker over the other and says:

She overdosed.

The old woman, Dorothy, has fallen asleep, and her puff of white hair moves softly with the air-conditioning.

You didn't ask, but I'm telling you. So you can't make me invisible.

And then we both look straight ahead into the mirrored darkness of the window that faces the parking lot through which he came, through which I came, and it is a strange view, because I face myself there, sitting three chairs down from the boy, but also, we face the field, together, the road, the lights of the city, and the darkness between.

I looked for her forever, he says.

I do not know if he means tonight, or if he has searched for this girl his whole life and only just now lost her.

She was supposed to meet me, he says, and she didn't show. I wonder if maybe I can use your phone? I lost mine. I need to make a call.

I hand him my phone.

While he waits for an answer, the boy goes to stand in front of the window and looks out at the single traffic light beneath which he appeared, and again he places the toe of one tennis shoe atop the other, that same motion, and I think, *Evan*. That is a thing Evan does. When he's unsure. When he doesn't know what will happen next, or he knows and it's something bad.

evan

Y ou make up a father. You pretend it's a game, so each time the man is different, because you make up the man to suit the person you are at the time. As you change, the father changes. He becomes what you need.

What can we use? asks V.

Whatever you can find. And the best father will win. The best one comes to life.

All right. Readysetgo.

You choose for your design a sharpness. Cholla legs and arms. Bittersweet beard, ditch-willow torso. You make a man of dirt and cactus and agave sap and find yourself knowing the face staring out at you.

V uses tumbleweed. Makes a father built for movement. Dandelion tufts lift on a breath of wind and leave even as she builds.

I'm done making.

Me too! I'm done!

We stand over our creations.

Scoring based on:

Lastingness, utility. Strength. Also funniness.

Lots of hand-pointing, explaining various parts. Who made the father most like the real one?

Who wins?

We award ourselves twin scores of 9.6 on the father-making scale.

That's dumb, V says after a minute. I wanted to win.

Which one would you choose?

Neither.

I don't know which one of us says that.

jude

Hello.
I'm sorry.
At the hospital.
No, I mean yeah, I'm fine. It's not me
hurt. I told you. It isn't me.
I carried her, I
picked her up and carried
her limp, she wasn't breathing all the
way across
town and no one would
stop, no one would.
I thought they would.
I thought we'd have time but no one came.
I don't know.

They won't let me back.
Not family.
I'm not hurt, I told you.

After the boy hangs up, he asks: Can I sit beside you?

No one ever asks my permission to sit beside me, so I say yes.

He is close to me now. Close enough for me to smell him. Clean, like shampoo.

The boy and I watch the television in silence. On the screen a chef is cooking and he has a beard almost to his knees and moves around an outdoor kitchen; around licking flames, he flips a spatula and smoke rises. A slab of beef is tossed on a grill.

They are somewhere in Argentina, far away from this American night.

Flame blackens meat. That looks delicious, I say.

That looks awful, the boy says. Can you answer me a thing?

What.

Where's the dad?

virginia

We walk together, my brother and I, we walk not too fast along this nice street, along the river. The path is paved and trees touch fingers over our heads. They are not scrubby cottonwood but big maples and willow and just on the other side of their branches is a gated neighborhood full of castles overlooking the river, and here is a playground with swings and a jungle gym. There is a pond littered with someone's leftover sandwich crusts, and a plastic baggie floats in the shallows. There is a cinder block building with bathrooms.

We slide beneath the upside-down green umbrella of the willow, peer between sprays.

Hello, we say to the tree and weave between ropy tendrils. A breeze lifts, then drops, long arms around us. The tree is bowing.

We bow back.

The tree says, Climb me.

I am careful of the littlest branches. I know what it is to be stepped on, to be small or snapped, even, so I kick off my sneakers and move lightly.

Maybe we can stay, I say.

We can, Evan says. Stay. He is climbing higher. We'll grow old, he says, reaching, and we'll have moss beards. We'll listen to water until we are calm. And our bones will grow and we will grow and the tree, everything growing together and we will be quiet here in the tree as it goes yellow with autumn. As it drops its leaves and gathers snow, thick and soft. And the snow will fall, white on the black river, and the spring will come again. And again and again. We will live here, happily ever after, tree twins.

Until we die.

What happens next?

When you die you fall out of the tree and into the earth.

Like a seed.

Yes but you got to live your life first.

Good evening, says a voice.

I freeze. I am afraid. It is like being afraid has swallowed me whole.

I didn't mean to scare you!

It is the army veteran from the park, the one who doesn't talk. He is on the bike path, a man with very large shoulders, pushing a shopping cart. He parks his cart in the wood chips beneath the swings.

He doesn't ask, What are you doing out alone at night or any of the ordinary things. I didn't mean to scare you! he says again. I'm sorry!

Our dad is watching us, I tell him. He lives in one of those houses. One of those big ones across the way, and he's watching.

The soldier nods.

He makes a lot of money, I add.

That's a very nice house, he says. Then he sits down, cross-legged beside his cart in the wood chips that smell a little bit of pee, a little bit of cedar. Pulling a blade of sweetgrass, he places the tender, pale stalk in his mouth. My name is Ernst, he says. He holds out his hand and shakes the air, like we are beside him. You like tree houses, free houses. I like movies.

I like movies too.

Nice to meet you. You can watch the movie from there, then, he says.

He's rummaging in his cart and I don't know what he means.

Would you like magic, he asks, or real?

I look at my brother. Real, I say.

Sure you want real?

Yes.

He laughs. Then takes some twine from the cart and loops it around two little trees planted by the city. The trees might not survive. There are little cages around their trunks. I tell him this. My cheek is pressed against the tree.

Maples are stronger than they look, he says. Lots of times they grow just fine where they're planted.

How old are you? Evan asks.

How old do you think I am?

He is looking up at us. His body and face are young and very strong, but there is something wrong with the eyes. Nineteen or a hundred, I say.

He laughs, and it is a boy's laugh. Boy-laughing old-eyed.

I decide I am not afraid. Sometimes I just know. I come down the tree and stand in the wood chips. What's next? I ask.

Now he takes out something like a cotton sheet—a screen, I realize—and clothespins. He passes me one and clips one end of the sheet to the line, and I clip the other end. He goes back and sets a projector on the tray of the cart.

That's a lot to carry around.

My favorite thing before I went to war was a drive-in. Everyone sitting together on the grass watching a movie.

What war?

It wasn't here.

We're not from here.

No, he says. You're not. You're from the trees.

Wars are never here.

True, he says.

Where was your war?

It wasn't mine. Far away, he says. You couldn't even imagine.

I want to try.

He nods. All right. One moment, he says. Just let me get this fixed up.

He has a long orange extension cord and he plugs it into the back of the cinder block building with the toilets and runs it into the back of his projector. While he does this, the leaves of the baby maples flicker gently in the beam of white light from his projector.

You had to worry about things exploding on you, he says, adjusting the beam. Sometimes big things. Sometimes things would end up in the wrong place. A car. A house. A school. Bricks and metal flying through the air regular as birds.

You don't like a roof, says Evan, who understands everything.

I like a sky, Ernst says.

He presses a button. On the screen appears the pixelated figure of a strange little man unlocking a bunch of drawers with a silver key and birds are flying everywhere! The little man on the screen has a mustache.

Who is that?

That's Charlie. The soldier lies on his back in the grass, propped up on his elbows, smiling and smoking something that smells not like a cigarette. That's my friend Charlie Chaplin. You know him?

No.

The film is in black and white, and his friend Charlie Chaplin just keeps doing what everyone says not to do, and every time, the result is something built out of wonder. He seems just as surprised as everyone else at this. Evan and me are doubled over, laughing. Evan and I sit in the swings to watch and bump each other in the dark. The laughing fills us up. When the credits start rolling, my mouth hurts from smiling.

Hey.

Yeah?

That wasn't real!

It was as real as anything else.

I told you a lie, I said. My dad, he isn't in that house. That isn't our house at all.

Ernst says, Right.

You want to know what my dad does?

Certainly.

He's an astronaut.

The soldier arranges his elbows and tilts his head back so he might look only at the sky, smoke still pluming from his mouth. He points solemnly up, past the silver images flickering on the sheet, and I am afraid.

That he will laugh at me.

He says, I think I see him, just there. Is that him? Next to the moon?

I nod. It is, I whisper, and there is my father, tiny and weightless and floating in a vast, dark space. We watch together.

He *is* watching over you. I can tell.

Thank you, I say.

The man Ernst packs up to go. I stand at the edge of the little park and wave as he leaves, pushing his cart. He pops a wheelie over a rut. He turns and waves back at us, then shoves the cart down a little hill and hops aboard, rolling with his head up and his back straight, all the way down the hill.

jude

He arrived at the apartment still wearing boots and long underwear. The seams of his hands were stained with oil. He knocked, and when I didn't answer he tried the knob, and when it turned for him, he came in and stood in my kitchen.

He'd not been there before.

The blinds were drawn. Dim slats of light striped the dirty dishes piled in the sink. There was a spatula with dried pancake batter beside the stove. He was studying the place thoughtfully as I came out of the bedroom and stood, leaning against the doorjamb. I wore a ratty gray T-shirt and no bra, his boxer shorts.

I tried to call, he said. And then: You look like shit.

My hair was loose, a knife part down the middle. I like it that way. It falls to my waist. Thanks, I said.

Then he said, You going to let me in?

You already let yourself in.

He knelt to unlace his boots.

You don't need to do that, obviously.

All right. I won't.

He stood with his boots still on and one unlaced.

Wow, he said.

Yeah?

The general aesthetic of the place is astounding.

I shrugged. He looked at my legs, long and bare. You haven't answered my calls, Jude.

I know.

Those are my boxers, he said.

Want them back?

Still got your sense of humor.

What do you want, Luke?

Thumbs in his pockets, he said: I want to know why you haven't been taking my calls. I mean, Jesus, Jude. You all right?

No.

You need a shower.

I know. I just can't be bothered.

When do those kids come home?

Three.

Come on then, he said, and lifted me. The surprise made me go very still against his chest and he held me there. I am not often held.

Luke said, Hey. He said he did not like the emptiness in my eyes. He said this softly, holding me against his chest. He said: Where's your bathroom? Just down that way, I said, through the bedroom to the right. He carried me down the hall. On the bathroom floor were towels, kids' bubble bath on the rim of the tub in pinks and yellows. He said: I'm going to have to put you down for a minute, OK?

OK.

Such gentleness.

He set me down and I sat weakly on the closed toilet lid while he started the shower and cranked the hot water all the way.

OK. This will feel good. Arms up.

I lifted my arms like a child, and he pulled off my T-shirt. Then he helped me to stand. Pulled his boxers from my waist and I stepped out of them. The sound of water falling. The clothes crumpled on the floor. Steam filling the bathroom. I stood before him naked and he placed his hands on either side of my ribs and then on the small swell of my stomach, and as I was looking at his hands on my skin I said, No, don't move them. He was still fully clothed, with his boots on.

You look like some kind of sexy water nymph, he said. Go on, get in. I stepped in the shower and he stripped of his shirt and left it beside my clothing on the floor. Bare-chested, he reached in and squirted shampoo in my hair, massaging it into my scalp.

Jesus, he said. You got a lot of hair. He wrapped it around his wrist, showing me.

Come in here with me, I said.

He stripped the rest of his clothes off—his boots and jeans—and washed me, the bar of soap white with froth. He held my hip and pressed against me, but that was all. There, he said. God, look at you. I never really got to see them in the light.

The tattoos.

He moved the bar of soap up the xylophone of my ribs. Floating bus stops and butterflies. In the shadows, a child kicking a dog. Beneath my scapula a soldier crouching beside a shopping cart, his shoulders draped in doves. Two front wheels of the cart peeling from the ground—the doves lifting the cart and the man—an unfolding feathered hand reaching down.

I don't understand it.

Every time I leave a place, I add something I saw.

You didn't see these things.

I did.

How many places you left?

I don't know.

C'mon, let's get you dry. He rubbed me with the towel and wrapped another around my clean hair and one around his own waist.

Where you keep your sheets?

I told him. He stripped the bed and made it up with clean sheets and I lay back against the pillows with the towel on my head.

When was the last time you ate something?

I don't know.

I'll make us some soup. I brought some for my lunch but there's more than enough.

He went out to his truck and got his thermos and came back in and reheated the soup, which had gone cold while he was up in the canyon, and while it was on the stove he washed our dishes in the sink and wiped the counters and threw out the rot in the fridge, placing the trash outside the door. He brought the soup bowls back and we ate in silence, sitting up in bed, spoons clinking.

I thought maybe I was in love with him.

Nobody likes to eat alone, he said.

Why are you being so nice to me?

I like you.

I don't know why. I don't even like myself.

It will go away, you know. That feeling.

What?

That feeling you have.

Somewhere far below was the sound of the river, a long exhale. I have always chosen to live by rivers.

What time is it?

I looked at the clock on the wall. Two. We have some time. I put the bowl beside me on the bedside table and touched the towel at his waist and he said: Maybe not.

Really? I looked down, maybe ashamed or embarrassed or even angry.

No, he said, it isn't what you're thinking. It's just that if you're going to ghost me again, I don't want to, I don't think.

You don't think?

He looked at me, considering. Well, he said, it's hard being a man. I might be convinced either way.

I laughed, the sound harsh and new in my throat, and he put his finger to my lips. Is it OK if I'm on top? I whispered, and he lay back with his arms behind his head, looking at me. Yeah, he said. That's OK with me.

He looked at me and I saw myself: my dark, swollen nipples, the smooth cleave of wet hair. He pushed himself all the way inside me at once. I clamped his shoulder. My other hand spread on the drywall behind him. He was all the way inside me. He paused, looked at his hands on my torso.

Sometimes I can't get the oil out, he said. It drives me crazy.

He held my hips and drew me all the way down on him and for a few minutes we didn't talk, just fucked roughly and quietly, and then he made a sound deep in his throat and came. He wiped himself off and I fell softly on top of him. He said, I'd better go, and I said, Yeah, you'd better. He stood and began to dress.

I can get groceries, he said.

Is that what you think I need?

I'd imagine so, he said. I'd imagine from the state of your fridge you need something for your kids to eat.

I don't really want your help.

He was pulling on his shirt. Seems like you just took it.

That was sex.

Was that what that was?

No, I admitted. But you don't need to hold it over my head.

I'm not, he said. He was dressed now. I don't know why you have to say it like that. If you need help, I can give it. I want to.

I told him men always thought maybe they could pick up things that fall apart. It was a talent they had, that talk.

Well, that isn't me, he said. He turned to the door, said, I'll pick up some groceries. No—don't say it. I'm going to the store anyways, it isn't any extra work for me at all. I'll leave them outside the door tonight after you all are asleep. Just text me when it's OK so I don't scare the kids.

Don't, I said.

You going to get up then?

That's none of your business, I said sharply, and he looked at me with that yellow-eyed gaze and said: You're good at breaking things up, aren't you?

Right. That's something I'm good at. Now go on, go, get out of my house. I don't need your help.

Oh honey, he said fondly. You've got some real fucking issues. I can't really help that too much. I'll bring groceries. They'll be outside. He kissed me on my clean hair and left.

virginia

We swing high, over the castles. I always wonder if I could get over the bar. Make a complete circle. Pumping is you lean back, shoot forward. Chains shriek. Underdog me! We lean back against the chains. I hurtle off the swing at the top and land, skidding in wood chips.

You'll break your legs, says Evan.

I say: Again.

We go opposites. When I go back, he goes forward! We time it just perfect.

The warm air has risen from the river and the night has pressed down a cloud. Air and cloud kiss over the water.

Under. Faster, faster, up! Up up up!

The chains screech.

Now! We catapult through air.

You OK?

It knocked the wind out of me, that last one.

Ready, says Evan. We should—

Yes. Let's go. The corner of the sky is pale, like skin.

jude

I drowse in the upright chair. I dream of boxes. I search a cardboard city full of jut and shadow, chasing a flicker of light inside caverns of boxes that go on and on forever. The little flicker is my children. I get down on all fours.

A child's hiding place, along the ground, an alley of cardboard and corner, of couch legs, baby-belly heavy dragging, so heavy on a sidewalk heaved up by cottonwood roots. Grasses all sprung up through the cracks. I croon and call.

They are very small, holding themselves with arms around knees.

Can I come in? I whisper.

No, says Virginia.

Yes, says Evan.

I make a space in the dream for myself. Heat rolls off their bodies. Cricket song. I hold one rough twin, one gentle. I smooth from their backs all nightmares.

We were pretending, says Evan, that this was a castle.

And I see they wear small crowns, woven of juniper and wild oak and the spare things of the desert.

Can you make this a castle for us? asks Virginia.

I reach out and gather a brick from the darkness.

Small, heavy miracle in my hand.

It can be done, I say. I set the dream brick down, find another, and another, stacking bricks into walls and placing them with the right weight and balance; I find my new good hands can pull building materials out of air, I can flutter wind into flags, direct water into a moat. A castle is what I will build for you, I say, and I send a drawbridge creaking down on its chains as the door to waking unfolds.

Open, open.

Between cracks in cardboard glint stars.

I hold out my new good hands, say: Isn't it beautiful? Isn't it?

They are gone.

virginia

I want it to work. I want to go to the same school every day and take the same bus. In the summer I want to teach the baby to make boats out of leaves and race them in the river.

jude

I am going to be sick, the boy says.

When he returns, his face is damp and flushed.

You all right?

No. He says: You look all full of secrets. It's because of the baby. Having a baby inside you must make a mystery of a person.

I don't know. When I was the age you are now, I was already pregnant.

He nods.

I told my mom. I don't know why. I never could tell her things. I should have taken care of it on my own.

What did she say?

I don't remember exactly.

Yes, you do.

She said: You little slut.

The boy leans forward and lowers his head and clasps his fingers behind his neck and his lowered cap of hair is chestnut dark. He says, That was cruel.

She was afraid. She thought I'd ruined my life. She called, made an appointment at the abortion clinic. She thought it was the right thing. The next appointment they had.

Jesus.

It wasn't that I was good, I tell him, or that I had a conscience. That's not why I did what I did.

Which was?

Had them anyway. I showed up for the appointment and there were all these geraniums. You know those red flowers? The ones that bloom in the winter? Like miniature trees. Woody, that sharp smell. They called me back and I went in, and I put on that paper gown and sat on the table while the doctor—she had a mole and a whisker, a whisker! Growing out of the mole! She talked to me about it—how it would go. She talked and the whisker moved while she talked and when she left the room to get whatever she needed to get I took off the paper gown and put on my jeans and my Led Zeppelin T-shirt and I walked out into the waiting room by all those geraniums and out the door. You know the crazy part? I was happy after that. They make me so happy.

It's the time of night when people talk about what matters. In the morning it will be different.

You don't have to avoid what makes you happy, says the boy. Not always.

He's right, of course.

So, the boy says, and smiles. He has a wide mouth. What else?

There is the awkwardness that fills a space between two people when they've shared something intimate and need to erase it quickly with something stupid or silly, but I don't bother. I don't have anything to say, so I let the moment widen and swallow us whole. Then the charge nurse arrives, standing there with her clipboard and series of forms.

There's a problem with your paperwork. Can you please read through and check your history and everything? You need to document the changes.

evan

We are in a grove of grandmother trees. Tufts of old man's beard drape the branches, and abandoned cabins scatter beneath cottonwoods. They look left-behind, like toys washed up on some current. Their roofs are like half-slid-off hats. There is an official-looking sign on a post: RESTORATION PROJECT: JUNE. On the picture is the little house in my hand. You can see where the fire came, how it licked up the walls, and I think about what the girl named Scout said, in the laundromat:

Fire or flood.

She knew.

No one can live in a place like this.

You can see its guts, says V.

Houses don't have guts.

I like the idea of it: a house with a heart and lungs, a pulse. But these houses are dead. One is even flattened, like some giant's hand came down and smashed it to bits. Whoever lived here, all they knew was taken. I imagine people standing outside, a red morning, watching it burn. Flames flashing in the deep. Tails of fire flicking out the windows and the doors.

Come on, says V. Come in here.

Between the planks of the walls fall blades of moonlight. Burdock bullies between floorboards. I wade six or seven steps—that's how long it takes to cross the whole house— through thick rustle. A soot-encrusted stovepipe keels over in a corner next to blankets. Black char rings the ceiling. Someone homeless has slept here. It is like being outside and inside at once.

Hello, Old House, says my sister.

It's strange, her voice inside here.

Look, Evan.

The wall that isn't burnt is covered with old newspapers and the yellowed pages of books. Rusted staples hold the paper in place.

It's a story.

When I wiggle a staple with a fingernail, the paper shreds easily. Beneath this story is another story. Beneath the words are more words, so if you peel one story up, another is there waiting. *Changes of shape, new forms, are the theme which my spirit impels me . . . he'd fallen in love with the sky. Icarus flapped his naked arms, deprived of the wings which had caught the air that was buoying them upwards* . . . And then an advertisement for hair tonic.

Suddenly all the bright bars of moonlight in the house disappear and it is just dark. I am starting to know it, the dark. I look for the door of the house—there is no door. The door is gone. I step in one direction. It is like moving through, stepping into nothing.

Maybe this is what it is to vanish. My father disappeared.

Maybe this is the thing I've been offered—maybe I will vanish.

I look for my sister and she is all the light come back and it is in her hair and I will never leave her. V, I say.

It won't work. We can't bring a baby here.

jude

C laws by Charlene returns to her desk, and I look down at my name. My Social Security number.

I can't, I say. Not again.

What's wrong? asks the boy.

And I fall apart.

Nothing, I say. This is the third time I've filled this out and I don't think I can again—that thing you were saying about being invisible, I understand it. I know what it is you meant. I feel it, sometimes. A lot. All the time, really. It's like the world happens outside of me.

I look at my reflection. The woman in the dark window sits among rooftops and streetlamps, floating on the floor of the city, and I say, more to her than to anyone else:

These are strange things to say to a stranger in a waiting room. All this talking I'm doing with you. I don't talk about myself. But it doesn't matter. I'll never see you again. That makes it easy, doesn't it? You're a stranger and I don't know your name and you will be gone in the morning. I have lost people. I will not lose them. I will not. This, this—I flap the clipboard—they're always asking me to fill things out! Like if I pin myself down, if there are enough facts about me *here*—

The boy says, Stop. May I? He is holding out his hand for the clipboard.

I hand it to him and he reads it.

This boy reads my life. He moves his eyes over the facts of it: unmarried, under-insured, unhoused. He reads all that has come before, the addictions and desertions and abandonment. The single income or not. There is so much that is *not*, there. He moves his eyes over these facts, and when he finishes reading the first page he reads the second, and then he flips to the third, and through all of this I watch, and when he's finished, I say, I've filled out so many of these things, and I've never seen anyone read them.

He presses open the metal clip at the top of the board and removes the top sheet. He has freckles of paint on his slender fingers. He lays the form with my name and my Social Security number on the table fanned with magazines and folds it in half, lengthwise. He tucks in the two corners so they hug center. A fuselage emerges. Long and narrow. He folds. A nose. Folds. Wingspan. His smooth forehead crinkles and concentrating, he pushes up his sleeves, and for a moment I think I see more paint flecks, but then I see the track marks.

He looks up at me over the little plane and my mind shapes the word *junkie*.

Simon, he says. That's my name.

This boy has eyes like the floor of a forest. He is a beautiful boy. Too delicate for this world. He pulls his sleeves down.

how do you take care of another person at all?

virginia

It's all right, Evan. Look—everything here finds a way to grow through what is broken.

jude

The boy drops the paper plane into my lap.

Go on, he says.

What am I supposed to do?

Fly it.

I don't know how.

His hands over my hands as we hold it. Look straight ahead—there. Now draw your arm back. Snap. Let it go.

I do, and in the air it is perfect.

On the carpet it looks like a broken bird.

That's how, he says.

He looks at the locked door leading from the lobby to the rooms and the rest of the hospital.

What's her name? The girl you brought in.

Corrina, he says. The way he holds the girl's name in his mouth is angled and delicate, as though he made it for himself.

What happened to her?

She was supposed to meet me, he says. I was making her something. He holds out his hands with their paint freckles in red, white, and blue.

What I'm telling you is a love story, he says.

He tells me how he met the girl, Corrina, at school. How she didn't fit in. Totally broken. You know the type, he says. You could see it right away. I wanted her right away. And when she left class early, I stood up too. I walked her home.

We got to know each other.

She stood between the wings—you know how on Fourth Street there's that graffiti of the wings on the side of the City Market and you can stand in the middle? She stood in the middle of the wings. Cliché. But I loved her already. Sixteen, and we're in love, and the love makes us lonely even walking beside each other. I remember exactly everything. It was the time of day when shadows lean heavy from the buildings. A kid cruised by on a longboard. I remember his leg, the way it moved in rhythm. The wheels on the skateboard crushed dogwood flowers on the sidewalk, and Corrina looked up at the blank face of an apartment complex and said, This one is me. I was thinking what it might be like to touch her under the sweatshirt.

Who's this, then? her mother said.

She fed us. Sent food around her table. I didn't eat—I was nervous, I wanted her mother to like me. They'd come up from Mexico City and spoke perfect English. Tortillas and black beans, elote, salsa fresca with sprigs of cilantro. Her littles—Corrina's sisters—all of them with her same gray-black eyes, eating, perched on the back of the couch, standing in the kitchen. They stuffed their cheeks. Brawled on the linoleum. Her mama watched, elbow-deep in suds. A whole jungle of ink on her—like you. The kitchen filled with the smoke of cast iron and tortilla-blister; and Corrina stood balanced on one leg by the stove flipping tortillas with her bare fingers; she was easy with me; they all were; it was a loud house—you know, filled with good noise. Once I looked up across the table at her, her mother said: Oh.

She saw already that I loved her.

Corrina finished and scraped her chair back. Where you gonna be, Corrie?

Oh, out, Mama. Onward and upward.

One of the smaller girls barnacled my leg. Corrina reached down and tickled her armpit. Release, ball and chain, she said and the little sister rolled away across the floor.

Corrina, said her mother.

Mama?

Take care of each other.

Later that night, she said, Shoot me up between my toes.

I told her, I don't know what it is you mean.

Here, she said. I'll show you. Can I? Sit behind me.

She relaxed back against my chest. We were at the park. I asked her: What's it feel like? And she said: Like everything.

She showed me how.

I felt the sky change, shaded in with a pencil—charcoal, smudged darkness. Later we would have identical topaz bruises. We looked at the city and it came alive, every window a starburst, and I thought, So this is how it is, to live.

Tonight, she didn't show.

It was weird. I knew in the back of my mind: There's Fentanyl in the city. It's hard to know. Well, we got into some things we shouldn't have. We made a history of ourselves. Didn't we? Once we started, there was no stopping us. Nothing like it. So anyways. That's the world. Isn't it? There're these rules—we make them up! They don't make any sense, but they're there, forcing us down. It makes it hard to breathe. Hard to break through to something better. Heroin did that for me. Showed me how to break through. I don't expect that to be a popular opinion or for you to understand. You can't understand unless you've tried. And you should never try. I found her just under the old railroad bridge that crosses Thirty-second.

That's what I wanted to give her: a bridge.

I was making a picture for her. Dropping the spray cans as I emptied them, and when I finished, I rapped down to pick them up. The cans. And that's where she was. She must have been watching the whole time. I saw right away that something was all wrong.

She was a scribble on the ground. I thought, She's asleep. But of course she wasn't asleep.

I picked her up—I picked her up and called out her name. She was right there in my arms but she couldn't answer she couldn't and she wasn't breathing, she was warm but wasn't breathing, so I cleared her throat and there was nothing there and I called emergency response. Someone answered right away. He said, What is your address? And I said, I think she's dead.

He said: Where are you? I need your address.

I said, She's dying. Tell me what to do.

And he left his script. He told me, Hold her heart in your hands.

I did the CPR like he told me. I did the counts. The phone tucked between my ear and shoulder and he stayed on with me. He told me exactly what to do. When to change. Her ribs cracked—I think I broke some. And he said: Now breathe for her. Give her your air. I did, and somewhere in the holding of her heart and the giving of my air the phone died between my ear and shoulder and fell into the rocks. I knew then. I'd fucked up so bad. I hadn't told him where we were. There was no one to save her but me, and I'm no good, and I thought, She's dead she's died here on these rocks and

I fucking didn't tell him where . . . The river. It was making that sound all around us and I kept going, I held her heart and then she whaled in air.

Just whaled it in.

I turned her head to the side, and she vomited. Two wet rivulets run straight back from the corners of her eyes into her ears, and I gathered her up—she didn't cry out.

I gathered whatever was left of her up.

I walked out from beneath the bridge with her in my arms. Into the street. The neighborhood gone strange. Surreal. Like a fucking monster held this city in its mouth and shook until it broke. I carried her past a construction site, wire coiled like veins in the walls. An off-duty taxicab passed us. It didn't slow or stop. I carried her past an old man with his back against a telephone pole; I don't know if he was asleep or maybe he was dead. I carried her—I patted her cheek. Open your eyes, Corrina.

You stay too long and things get complicated. We should have left it there, me and her, in the kitchen. The end, he says. Unfinished.

evan

D rop the tiny house on the ground. Step on it. Smash
it. Like it was nothing to you at all.

virginia

WHy did you do that?
Because it was stupid.

No, it wasn't, Evan.

He says: It was. It was just pretend, and I think: We can't stay here. We don't have anywhere else to go.

Evan. What will we do now?

Go home.

Where is that?

I don't know.

Back the way we came. Back by the castles that have new windows with stickers still on them.

Evan, do you feel like those windows are eyes? Like someone is watching?

He picks up a rock. His throw is perfect. Plate glass caves.

I can make it eyeless, he says.

I get my own rock.

The houses sit quietly. We are methodical. House to house, window to window, we leave shards of glass on new concrete. The reflection in the shards rearranges the way you think of the moon.

Evan.

What?

I'm scared of the dark.

He says: There's nothing in the dark that isn't in the light too.

We walk along a frontage road between trees. The sound of our steps are lonely in the clear darkness.

V? I wonder if you'll be like her. When you grow up.

I hope not.

I hope so.

jude

The night we moved here we drove along the river, the whole way, passing through each small town beaded like a necklace along the banks of the river, and somewhere on the long highway all the bars on the cell disappeared, and the plains opened before us and greened. I take them to rivers often. There are many things wrong with me. But I can give a child a river, no problem at all. That day we pulled into a dirt parking lot by the railway bridge. I told them we'd go down, eat our peanut butter sandwiches. We would like to know about our dad, they said.

What did you say? The boy sits beside me in the waiting room and listens. Time is out of joint. I do not know how long I've been here.

I told them he was good at pictures.

Did he do this one?

The boy points to the ink on my wrist, Icarus.

Yes, I say.

He was good. I don't know my father. But I think that is a job a dad might do. A father might leave you one good thing.

He left me two. I told Evan, You are like him, in that way. The making of your pictures. And Virginia, the way you don't stop moving? You are like him too.

How did he die? asked Virginia.

I said: I am trying to tell you how he lived.

That's not the question, Evan said.

I don't think it's something you need to know. It's hard to understand.

They looked at me. There was the smell of the river, damp, growing, and Virginia said: We want to try.

He fell. One day we were in love. We were on a roof. We were messing around. And he fell.

That's all?

Yes. He was there one minute, and then he was gone.

Jesus, says the boy.

Do you want to see a picture of them? My twins?

Yes.

I take out my phone.

Here they are.

The boy takes his two fingers and places them on the screen and spreads them wide, expanding the image. He studies their small faces. Then he shows me how you can see, if you look closely, little dirt nests clinging to the underside of the bridge where tiny birds with little pointed wings live.

Swallows live in places people are happy, he says.

evan and virginia

We will cross the railroad bridge on foot because you cannot get a river to carry you upstream. A river only goes the way it wants. And we are like the river. We are going home. When we get to the railroad tracks we give our ears to cool steel, to listen.

When the train crosses this bridge and passes over the river, it will drag morning behind it.

The sound strums our bodies. A mechanical heart. RATATATATATATAT.

jude

I close my eyes and behind my eyelids are the white patterns reminiscent of snowflakes. One morning not long ago a spring snowstorm came in the night. I woke to the buzzing of the phone. School—cancelled. I was called off the restaurant. The kids and I stood at the window in pajamas.

The world had gone glittering. Treacherous. Ice had dragged powerlines to sidewalks. Black crows raucous against a sky as white as sheet music, crows like notes on a staph.

Virginia, Evan. Get your boots on.

I led them out into the raw, bright-white day. We hiked above the town and into the lemon orchard encased in ice. Evan said: Beneath the snow there are yellow suns. They swished around in snow pants. Dug holes. Built forts and pummeled each other with snowballs. I reminded them it was not nice to add gravel bits to the outside as spikes.

Virginia trucked back and forth across the orchard, ruining the perfect white blanket. Their mouths and cheeks bright red, noses running. I was sleepy and sitting, warm against a tree.

I'm *bored*, Virginia said.

To be still has always made her itch.

We should play a sitting-still game because Mama is so tired, said Evan, and I told them, I'm fine, and Virginia said, Games like that aren't any fun, and Evan said, You don't have to play, then, and Virginia said, Fine I won't.

Two minutes later she threw her body up from the snow angel she was making, back and forth and forth and back; angels were boring too, she said, and asked: What was that game again?

Thought you didn't want to play.

The NAME of the GAME!

Awright, awright. Things You Are Afraid Of.

I'll tell one first—

And *then* we do magic, Evan said. To get rid of it.

OK. Mama, you first.

I looked at that pretty girl and pretty boy that were mine. I tried to keep my traitor fingers from reaching out to touch their cheeks. That would annoy them.

Stop eating that snow, Virginia.

It has dog pee in it, actually, said Evan.

Virginia said, I am afraid of—

Coward! belted out Evan.

Evan! Shut up!

Aw, I'm just kidding. Mom first.

I'm not playing.

M-*om*.

It's hard to explain, I said. Isn't it? Fear.

The orchard sat high on a ridge, and we looked down over the river. Against the snow it was completely black and still. Like silk.

It's hard for me to tell you, I said, but I guess what I'm afraid of is losing.

What kind of? The question sat there, barbed, in the air.

Losing you two. Losing me, too. I'm not good at thinking about it. It's like . . . I frowned and pushed a hand out into white air.

To keep it away, said Evan.

Yes. I'm not good at thinking of it.

No one is.

Hopeless at thinking of it. But it's there all the time.

So don't do it, said Evan. Don't ever think about it.

Or don't lose us, said Virginia.

Your turn, Virginia.

Yeah, yeah. What about you, V?

The dark.

That's a *baby* fear, said Evan.

I can be afraid of what I like. You don't get to tell me.

I was looking into black branches. The crows were talking, and I didn't want to play anymore.

V? said Evan, thoughtfully. I bet you aren't scared of the dark. You're scared of *people* in the dark.

And she's right to be, I said. She should be.

They both stared at me. Go play, I said.

The lemonless lemon tree above me sorted sky. Ancient and gnarled and each black branch decked with snow. For a while I slept inside the winter chattings of gray jays. I dreamt of flight. Not flying but wanting to. I dreamt I was enfolded in a pair of wings. My plumage the color of gunmetal. Cold feathers brushed my face. I woke and it was snowing again. I dug down, below the snow, and scraped a thin layer of black soil with my fingernail. I put it to my tongue. It was what I wanted.

It was snowing hard, very fat, fresh flakes, and I saw what my children were doing.

Evan stood in front of Virginia. The girl had something tied around her eyes—his shirt. He was bare-chested in the snow, his back curved like a fishhook, chest puffed out. Little nipples like knots. He called out to his sister looking for him in the dark. Virginia's arms stretched out; he was talking her through. She was falling, and catching herself, and crying out with the laughing, and then he was holding her wrists. They walked around, him in the bright white and her in the dark, together, bumping into things and giggling. Banishing the fear, I thought. Doing the magic.

Come here, I called. My words took shape. It's too cold, I thought, for him to be without his shirt.

Hey, I'm sorry, I said. Come back.

virginia

I run. When I run, the earth cries out to meet me.

Up, rock-clambering; cattails blade bare calves, heel around the foundation, up and up, the bridge above; boom bar lowering and there breaking through the rushes is the iron face.

The train! I scream. It's coming!

Simmer, V, says Evan, but my mouth is open and laughing and my feet are jigging in gravel.

I can't help it!

There is no sense in talk, we're inside it, the morning; the head of the sun crowns the river and the train flies by, inside my chest a gnash of metal, spark, and sizzle as the train eats the tracks, trailing its long plume of dark smoke; running beside it, I lean into the noise and holler, cup hands around my mouth and make a megaphone, *Dingdingding* goes the alarm, and I can't hear myself inside the noise.

evan

Tourists sit in the open train cars holding steaming cups of coffee. A woman wearing bright red lipstick holds a paper cup. From the side she looks like our mother, with her black-black hair. I want to call out to her, Good morning!

It is a good morning. Today belongs to you. It is your birthday, and the sky swings open.

The woman sips her coffee, leaves a bloodred imprint on her paper cup. As she looks at V, her lipsticked mouth snaps down and she turns a sculpted cheek away and says a word. It is only one, but I know the shape of that word on a mouth.

What? says V. And is stilled.

What did she call us?

The woman is already gone. The train is a great swish and shush of metal rending steel, the stink of coal smoke, and beside me V lifts her shirt, tucks it under her chin and beats her naked chest. I am shouting, Stay back. You're too close. V takes another step and gathers every bit of spit in her throat and launches it at the train.

I tackle her.

I didn't like the way she looked! I didn't! Her screams hit my face, hot.

Calm *down*.

Did you hear what she called us? Did you see how she looked?

What, V? How'd she even look?

At us! You know! You know!

No, I don't! I didn't hear.

You're lying. Stop pretending, Evan Woods. Tell the truth! You heard.

Trash, I say. She called us trash.

She goes still. Her hair is loose and eyes green against gravel.

I hate her, she says. I *hate* that she lets this happen.

Climbing, at least, is easy. You push off the ground, then leave it behind. Trust your feet, sort what is ahead with fingertips. Your fingers crimp metal. Press your whole body to rust, bolt. Your skin scrapes hard against green paint, your eyes fear the river so far below, but still, you hoist up and up and up, punching your head into sky.

jude

All this night my body has been gathering in ferocity. In pain. And now the bearing down. The mouth of some malevolent God closes, jaw grinding, and I go hands-knees to the carpet. There is the smell of ocean in the room. My water breaks.

Oh God, says the boy.

Arch.

Pant.

Everything acutely drawn. A line of chairs. An amoebic screensaver dances across the computer at the empty reception desk. Above, the television flashes: FAT, as on the screen a chef wanders the belly of a slaughterhouse, winding between sides of beef, rib cages hooked and hung.

My spine liquifies.

crowning

The Sleepless Man is rolling a cigarette when a call comes in from an out-of-town number: an unattended child is climbing the railway bridge. His tobacco is loose, and fragrant. He listens, pinching the white paper from the package, sifting brown leaves down the middle. He licks the paper, rolls, and takes in smoke. The radio spits out some more words.

It is his. The call.

Later he will wonder at his next, slow, deliberate motions. How he considered stubbing out the roll-up in the tin can beside him and decided against. How after he rose from the stoop, he took time to stretch.

Hanging beside the door on a hook are his keys. He skirts the broken things on the sidewalk to get to the old pickup and turns the key in the ignition. The truck coughs to life. He backs up, then puts her in drive, rattling over the cattleguard.

Holding the steering wheel with his knees, he smokes, and at the bus stop blinkers left.

When he pulls into the parking lot at the base of the bridge, the first thing he sees are swallows, dipping and gliding up the pink ropes of dawn. The river holds the morning in it—people don't know that's how morning comes. From the river. It is only then he sees the boy in the sky.

Simon kneels to meet Jude's pain. His face is so close to her face: she sees he has very soft brown hair. The top of his left ear tapers to a slight point and there is a freckle on the lobe, and Jude sees him clearly now, his pure skin and green veins, the small scatterings of freckles across his nose like the footprints of some delicate wild creature in snow.

Oh, it hurts, she says.

I'm here.

Don't go.

I won't.

Simon keeps his eyes on hers. There's a lot of gold in them. The eyes of a wildcat. He thinks of Corrina and in his chest feels the pain that is like no other pain, that loss so imminent. In Jude's eyes are flecks of gold and fight.

It will be beautiful. After, she says. Oh it hurts. It hurts.

Simon yells, Fucksake! Someone come and help, it's time!

*   *   *

You're very high up, the Sleepless Man says to Evan. Here is what is going to happen. You are going to lean toward me. I'm going to count to three. And then, on three, you are going to let go.

I can't, says Evan. Never has he doubted his own certain, perfect balance—but now he knows. You can fall. It happens all the time. He looks at his hands and they are small and the railing is big and the water is far and it is fast below.

I'm afraid.

I'm going to catch you.

How do you know I'll fall the right way?

Because, says the Sleepless Man. Because I am here, says V, and just for a moment it is too much and Evan closes his eyes.

Wet cut light. Jude gleams. She is all pounding heart, she is all thrust. In another hospital room, the old, old woman in the wheelchair, she has forgotten her own name; what does it matter, anyway, her name? She lifts her dandelion-blown head. A slight striation, vibration? Outside the window just barely pale. It is time, she says, to water my roses.

Jude cries, I need to push—

Don't! The Sleepless Man leashes his voice. Don't do that, please. Eyes open the whole time. Because he does not like how small the hands, how big the rail, how far and fast the river. That river is rough, it is swollen with snowmelt, the current smashes against the shore.

They cage Jude in a bed with wheels and the doctor says: Lock the sidebar into place.

She rattles the rail. Now they run a needle into her spine and so she floats, into a white room, a window, a little square opening out into dawn-dark, see-search for them. *Find them find them* . . . Check in on the blue car in the field, she says to the nurse who holds her hand tight-tight.

Hold tight, the nurse says, and smooths the hair from Jude's forehead.

The blue car!

The nurse says: There, there, dear, it's the medicine.

Now the Sleepless Man throws both arms up like a prayer. There is no shortage, The Sleepless Man thinks grimly, of broken things in this world—only tonight, earlier, a lost boy called him about a girl whose heart had stopped under the bridge, she did it to herself, as though there are not enough things in this world to ruin a heart. Who knows where that girl ended up, he should have made the boy tell him the address—but now here is this girl. This small, golden-headed child on the ground beside him that touched his eyelids earlier and said *You are good*; he will give her back her brother—this shadow twin of herself, straight-backed and perched up in the dawn like a bird, fragile-boned and ruffled.

Hold on, he says. One.

We are twins in sky-pieces, thinks Virginia.

Oh! It is hard to breathe—The cord, says the doctor. Quickly now, the cord is wrapped—and Jude thinks, The rules were made before I started, I stretched myself as far as I could and ran as fast; I never had any idea what happens next; I wasn't given clues; once you've made up your mind to do a thing, you just go—

Doctor lays hands upon her great swelling. Now, come back. There. Ease up on that a little. Jude? We lost you for a minute. We're going in to get the baby now.

Her body under his gloves. Tattooed black grasses thread her abdomen, waiting to be severed, ink twines against the white sheet. To the attending he says: Don't rush.

Two, says Virginia.

Don't rush, says the Sleepless Man.

Evan thinks: There has never been anything but rush in us, and lets go of the railing.

They hang a sheet, so Jude's top half is separated from her lower, so she cannot see their knives. An antelope peels from the tattoo on her back, tucks legs beneath bright body and leaps, gamboling about the room. Pressure. Nostril flare. Black-horned, she lifts her head. Her throat opens, fills with scream. So cold, she thinks. The whole room brightens, there is too much light—

snick, quick we arch. Split. The child breach, fin-like, slick-sliding. Reach to catch the rising cry.

the park watches

T he two children climb out of the Sleepless Man's pickup
truck and sit on the step beneath the eviction notice.
Elbow to elbow, knee to knee.

After a while the girl rises and picks up a shard of
something.

Be careful, V. You'll cut yourself.

I won't.

Wait. I'll help.

Small hands sweep bits and pieces of wreckage. They pluck
crockery and grass from dirt. Shuttle fragments to the dump-
ster. The kitchen table is knocked to its side, legs sticking
out; they right it. The boy unwraps three newspaper-stuffed
coffee cups and sets them on the table. Each child takes an
end of the broke-backed yellow couch; they straighten it.

Very methodical, these two. Bent black-and-gold heads. They sort the silverware into a plastic holder. Forks on top of forks, spoons cupping spoons. The boy retrieves a pillow and smacks off dust. They each take an end of an old quilt, square the corners.

Come apart, move together.

The boy places an end table beside the bed in the street and the girl puts sheets on the bed. They run an extension cord to the outlet on the street pole, and click on the lamp.

The girl sits on the edge of the bed. The boy beside her. Then they tip like block buildings onto the single pillow. The boy places a hand in the space where her neck meets her collarbone and she tucks her chin to keep it there, and in the clean, clear voices of children out of earshot of adults, they speak of the night. Finally they close their eyes.

The birds are awake. Now there are stirrings in kitchens, coffeepots waft out their bitterness. A door shuts. Some stand at windows. A car starts but does not leave, idles.

The park watches the two children asleep in the yard.

When the locksmith arrives with his black bag, at first no one moves. Then the Sleepless Man rises from his stoop and picks up the gun.

The park watches as he crosses the space between 563 and 564. He climbs the single step and crumples the eviction notice in his fist. Then he returns to stand over the sleepers. He sets the gun gently down. Picking up the quilt, he unfolds all their careful folds and tucks in a sky twin and an earth twin.

One by one they come. Someone brings a gallon of milk. Someone else, coffee. A blanket. A loaf of bread. These things are laid on the table in the yard and people take up occupancy in the chairs and on the sofa. The group at the table shuffles a deck of cards. Someone offers the locksmith coffee. A blonde and a black head face each other on the pillow, foreheads leaning in, to touch. The sleep of children is a perfect thing.

In the hospital Jude Woods undoes her gown. The baby's mouth a blossom, working the nipple. She breathes in the scent of milk. Peat. She pulls the sheet up and over them both and makes for herself and her child a roof.

Acknowledgments

I 'd like to thank my editor Elisabeth Schmitz for her generosity, artistry, and belief, and for the expansive effect those qualities have on my work. Thank you to Laura and the incredible team at Grove. I am so grateful to my agent, Jennifer Lyons, who championed this story from the beginning and reminds me that I just need to write as well as I can, and she will take care of the rest, which she does with incredible energy. I would like to thank the Elizabeth George Foundation, the Aspen Foundation, and Lighthouse Writers Workshop for their generous support while I wrote this book. I'm indebted to the genius of Debra Allbery and Ellen Bryant Voigt for my apprenticeship at the Warren Wilson MFA program, and my mentors: Peter Turchi, Dean Bakopoulos, Karen Bender, Sarah Stone, and Dominic Smith, among many others—thank you to each of you. I could not have written this book without my dad, Richard, who taught me that people are inherently good, and that if you take care of a piece of land, it will take care of you. I am grateful to my mom, Evan, who secured in me a deep and abiding love of reading. And thanks to my brother, with whom I shared a wild childhood. To the many young writers I've worked with over the years: your stories have taught me that hope, courage, and kindness are our natural state. Thank you.

Finally, thank you to Althea and Sean. Love is fierce and constant in this house, and it is everything.